What people are saying about Jenny Gardiner's books:

Red Hot Romeo

"Awesome". So enjoyed the romantic chemistry between the two characters. Read it non stop into the wee hours. Highly recommend this book
-- Mrs. K

Blue-Blooded Romeo

"Another brilliant, fun read from Jenny Gardiner. The book is fun to read and I thoroughly enjoyed every word. Jenny Gardiner has put the fun back into romance books and I look forward to each book in this delightful series."
-- Anne Blyth

"I had planned on only reading a few chapters at first but couldn't put it down. A terrific storyline, well-developed and extremely relatable characters, what's not to love?? Great read!"
-- Samantha Reeves

Big O Romeo

"I could not put this book down. Warning don't start this book late at night as you will not want to stop reading.
 -- Di

Sleeping with Ward Cleaver

"A fun, sassy read! A cross between Erma Bombeck and Candace Bushnell, reading Jenny Gardiner is like sinking your teeth into a chocolate cupcake...you just want more."
 --Meg Cabot, NY Times bestselling author of Princess Diaries, Queen of Babble and more

Slim to None

"Jenny Gardiner has done it again--this fun, fast-paced book is a great summer read."
 --Sarah Pekkanen, NY Times bestselling author of *The Opposite of Me*

Falling

for

Mr. Wrong

(book one of the Falling for Mr. Wrong series)

by Jenny Gardiner

Chapter One

IF Harper Landry got stuck with one more blind date who was yet another prime candidate for Loser of the Year, she might punch the guy. Yeah, yeah, she knew that wasn't a particularly charitable notion. After all, the succession of men she'd agreed to date for a variety of idiotic or mercenary reasons clearly couldn't help themselves—they were pathetic specimens of their species. It wasn't fair to kick someone when they were down, was it? And no doubt, some of these guys were down in the dumps. Then again, surely they could work to amend some of their more regrettable personality traits.

Like the guy who—before their appetizers had even arrived—started sobbing about his fiancée who'd ditched him. Nine years ago. That was the most depressing date she'd had in ages. Not only was it a waste of her time—and money, since he insisted they go Dutch—he also put her on speed dial just to bawl to someone he thought gave a care. Because she stupidly expressed empathy for his sorry self. Harper felt all the more foolish—she'd donned false eyelashes for the occasion, optimistically thinking it would brighten up her face. Hell, she could've worn a potato sack and that dude wouldn't have noticed.

Then there was the guy who kept spitting on her face

as he badmouthed pretty much every person he spoke about. While drinking himself under the table. She'd never forgive the organist from her mother's church for roping her into that unfortunate night on the town with her beloved nephew. Particularly when he vomited at her feet as he got into the taxi she insisted on hailing for him when he was too drunk to drive.

Perhaps there was something seriously wrong with her that she couldn't discern on her own. Harper didn't want to be vain or anything, but from where she was looking, she was under the impression that she was perfectly fine and normal and pretty and nice. Or at least she presumed as much.

She took a look in the mirror as she readied herself for yet another date with destiny—more like a date with desperation—and forced a smile as a sort of spirit-boosting maneuver. After a couple of reinforcing self-affirmations— *I am kind, I am smart, I am friendly, I deserve respect and happiness*—she ran her fingers through her auburn waves, which she thought looked more than acceptable. That certainly couldn't be a deal breaker with a man. Besides, her hair was more brown than auburn if she was going to be truthful about it. No guy hated brown hair, did he?

She then practically pressed her face to the mirror, trying to see if she had some particular facial flaws that might turn a guy off. Nope. She always took pride in her exquisite sea glass-green eyes, which were cat-shaped in a way. They made her look mysterious. But maybe men thought they made her look too feline, too elusive? Wait a minute. Because of her eyeballs? That would be so stupid. She wouldn't want to be with a man who was so ocularly judgmental (and was ocularly even a word?).

With a tug of her dress, she smoothed it with the palm

of her hands where it bunched a little bit along her hips, then turned sideways. Well, damn! She looked amazing if she did say so herself. She had an attractive figure, a beautiful set of legs—and the heels she was wearing only made them look better. So why, oh why, if she wasn't a scraggly, sad-sack loser with bad breath (oh no! was her breath bad?), was she stuck dating such a rogue's gallery of the lamest men this charming little beach town she loved had to offer?

Could it be her personality? Again, she didn't want to be cocky, but as far as she could tell, her friends all thought she was normal. And nice. And funny. Funny was good, right? But did guys think funny was too, like, Seth Rogan, for a girl? Was being funny supposed to be only the domain of raunchy, paunchy comedians? Did guys hate a girl who was a little sarcastic, who loved to crack a good joke? Maybe they didn't like that she sometimes used salty language. After all, she rarely met a good f-bomb she wasn't happy to detonate. Under the appropriate circumstances.

That would be super hypocritical, though. Any guy would be all over it like white on rice if she talked like that while having sex with them. Didn't guys love that? All "Fuck me, baby," and "Oh, yeah, I fucking love when you do that," and "Oh, your fucking cock is so big," and such. Hmmm, maybe she needed to up the ante in the naked dirty-talk department. But then again, as it was, she wasn't getting anywhere near naked—she wasn't even graduating to the kissing stage—because ugh, given the guys she'd been dating, she'd just as soon never shake the sheets again than compromise her standards by sleeping with those lackluster specimens. She'd settle for her trusty pocket rocket any day over that.

She grabbed her phone and checked the time on it, then ordered up an Uber and went to the curb to wait for it. This way if the date was as horrible as they usually were, she could get stinking drunk and not worry about driving home. All the more important as she was meeting her mystery date—Danny Greevy, a friend of a friend of a friend's friend's uncle's goddaughter, or something like that—at a new restaurant several towns over, so even farther from home.

She'd honestly lost track of most of these forgettable men at this point. Why, she wondered, did she continue to show up for the dates, hopeless as they always were. Her optimistic streak far outpaced her reality, but sometimes hopeful was all you could hang your hat on in this world.

When the driver dropped her off at the designated address, she straightened her dress, wiped a smudge of lipstick off of her teeth she'd noticed when she glanced in the rearview mirror, and stepped out of the car. Only to behold her destination: an actual restaurant called Octopussy. Lord help her. The regrettably named dining establishment featured a mammoth three-dimensional female octopus, whose bulbous body erupted from the top edge of the building like a zit that needed to be popped. Her eight human-style legs (ending in stilettoed feet, of course) extended around the edges on either side of the establishment as well as down the front wall. Harper was surprised there wasn't an exposed vulva and a bush of pubic hair to further make the point. Though no doubt this octopussy would be waxed clean.

She slowly walked the path to the restaurant as if a pirate held a cutlass to her back to force her down the gangplank. To be truthful, she'd probably have been more enthusiastic about that. At least maybe the pirate would be personable, or—better yet—a little lustworthy if she were lucky.

Ugh. This place bore all the hallmarks of a strip club, which was why she was taken aback when she opened the door and was greeted by a tuxedo-clad maître-d'. *Okay…*

"Um, I think I'm meeting my date here." Harper tucked her hair behind her ear, a nervous habit that gave her something to do while she debated fleeing.

She scanned the restaurant and finally "got" the theme—it was some retro James Bondesque thing, and the place had all sorts of spy-type paraphernalia framed and mounted on the walls. Kind of like how Applebee's might have antlers or old-timey pictures from the heartland or faux tin Pennzoil signs everywhere, only instead it was guns with silencers attached and pictures of James Bond's getaway cars and an autographed picture of Roger Moore in his heyday. Weird.

"Miss?" The host lifted a questioning eyebrow.

"Landry. Harper Landry. I'm meeting Danny, um"— she pulled out her phone and opened her calendar to find the guy's name again—"Greevy. That's it, Danny Greevy."

Harper heard the door open behind her.

"Danny Greevy at your service," she heard a voice say behind her. She turned to see a man bent at the waist in a bow. He stood up and reached for her hand. "You must be the delightful Harper Landry I've heard so much about. And you're even more beautiful than I was led to believe."

Harper tried to suppress a grin. This guy had potential. First off, he appeared to have manners, which was nothing to shrug off. Especially considering one of her recent dates let the door slam on her face when they left a restaurant at the same time. The glass of the door literally hit her in the nose. Needless to say, they went in opposite directions once outside. Secondly, yowza. He was pretty damned hot. His dishwater-blond hair seemed to fall into place from its side part as if following orders. Warm brown eyes and a dimple in his left cheek completed the picture.

Wait a minute. She did a mental double-take. Something was awry here. The guy was cute and polite. There must be something wrong with him. Alas, she knew she'd have all evening to discern what his fatal flaw was. And she'd sure as hell figure it out.

Chapter Two

TWENTY minutes into the date and no flaws were jumping out at her. Instead, he kept inching up the "potential" list. Go figure. Granted he was pretty much the only guy on it. Add to his attributes: an unexpectedly charming sense of humor. Turned out Danny had hoped that Harper would get a good laugh out of a restaurant named Octopussy. That was good news on two fronts: one, he actually *had* a sense of humor. And two, he obviously delighted in a woman who shared such with him.

"I figure if a date shows up here and storms off, she's not for me," he said as the waiter handed them each a menu. "It's always the easiest way to weed out the stuck-up ones."

"Stuck-up?" Harper lifted her eyebrow. "That's not usually the ones I'm contending with. Instead most of my blind dates are developmentally stunted. Like they've spent the better part of the last five years hunkered down in their parents' basement playing video games. They have that pasty-white flesh, they're usually a bit out of shape, and most of the time they're sorely lacking in basic social skills."

Danny shook his head as he ordered a bottle of wine for them both. "I suppose the women I tend to end up with on first dates would be an upgrade from that. But not by much. Mostly they're first and foremost after a ring and a lifetime commitment. Usually by the time dessert is served. They tend to laugh a little too hard at my jokes, fawn over me like a doting grandmother, and treat me like some delicate endangered species—*a single male!*—the dodo bird of this century."

Harper held up her hands in surrender. "Trust me, there will be no pretense of that from me. I'm happy to go on a few dates, but I am decidedly not in search of some elusive 'Mr. Right.'" She made air quotes. "After some of the dates I've been fixed up with, I'd be perfectly happy with Mr. Have Some Fun." In hindsight, Harper thought perhaps that wasn't the best way to phrase that, but she figured correcting herself would only draw attention to the wayward comment, so she let it go.

"Well then, we'll get along just fine." The corners of his mouth turned up, his perfectly straight white teeth bared in a smile.

He truly was such a handsome man.

"You up for some dancing?" Danny said as they chatted over coffee after dinner.

"Where?"

Danny pointed his thumb behind him. "There's a whole other section of this place that's more like a nightclub."

Harper tipped her head in disbelief. "Here? On the sleepy North Carolina shoreline, there's an actual nightclub I've never heard of?"

"Hard to imagine you're a local and didn't know of it."

"Like I said, the extent of my social life has been going out to the Olive Garden with the godson of Aunt Gertrude or the nephew of Mabel, the church organist, so dancing hasn't been high up on my, uh, dance card." She grinned.

"Then we'd better make up for lost time."

Danny stood and pulled Harper's chair out, then linked arms with her to escort her to the club.

He led her down the hallway, past the doors to the restrooms and the kitchen, where there was an unmarked door. He opened it, ushering her through it into what seemed like a large speakeasy, where a jazz band was playing big band music. Danny pressed his hand to her lower back as he led her to the dance floor, where he grabbed her hands and they started dancing.

Harper could still not get over that there was a nightclub a mere twenty minutes or so from her house. She lived in a small beach community, and while there were plenty of things to do nearby, they often entailed the typical cliché beach activities like putt-putt golf, drive-in movies, or all-you-can-eat seafood restaurants. This was downright exciting.

"I love to dance," she said as Danny grabbed her hips and moved along with her. Soon a slow song came on and he pulled her closer. Harper could feel him pressed to her hips and knew he was aroused. Wow. A man. Turned on by her. Downright shocking.

She wondered why that was such a stunning turn of events. Was it her lack of confidence that had led her to the drought she'd been in for so long? Inevitably her thoughts always went down the same path when she started to ruminate on this problem. It all came back to Noah Gunderson. The one who broke her heart when he left her so unexpectedly, right when she thought they were heading toward a lifetime together. If anything chipped away at her self-esteem, that was it. So while she wasn't one to hold a grudge, if there was anyone she'd maybe still consider slugging were she ever to run into him again, it would be Noah.

Thank goodness he left this place years ago. With any luck, she'd never see him again.

"Would you like to come back to my place for a nightcap?" Danny whispered into her ear as they slow danced.

Nightcap? That sounded like something a pickup artist would say. It had been a long damned time since Harper had a "nightcap." Or even a daycap for that matter. Daycap. Maybe that would be called "afternoon delight." Crap. She hadn't had that since, well, since that cursed Noah. Three days before he took off for parts unknown, leaving her high and dry and wondering what was so wrong with her that a guy would up and bail like that after being together for so many years. No wonder she struggled to feel value when it came to men. The man she thought treasured her had discarded her like an old tissue.

Nightcap indeed. It was time to take the bull by the proverbial horns and have herself a fun little nightcap with Danny Greevy.

"A nightcap sounds perfect." She winked at him.

As they walked away from the dance floor, she pulled up the Uber app on her phone and called for a driver, who was there in four short minutes.

It had started to rain while they were in Octopussy, and Danny offered his suit jacket for Harper to cover her head with as they walked to the curb. Such chivalry. Danny was a keeper. She tried to ignore that nagging voice in her head asking if he was, then why wasn't he already kept?

When the car pulled up, Danny opened the door and helped Harper into the car. She scooted over to the far side and fastened her seat belt. A few cars drove past as she waited for Danny to buckle his, their lights refracting across the raindrops on the car windows.

Danny leaned over and kissed Harper on the nose. "I'm so glad you're coming over to my place. I want you to meet my cat."

Cat? Huh. What an unusual come-on, she thought. Though at least she didn't tell him she wanted him to meet *her* cat! Now that would be a little too strong of a come-on.

"Good evening, folks," their driver said as he punched in some data into the GPS on his dashboard-mounted phone. "We'll get you to Cutler Beach in no time."

Harper bristled. That voice. As much as she'd hoped to forget that voice, the minute she heard it, she felt a chill lift the hair on her arms. She'd know that miserable rat-bastard voice anywhere.

"Noah?"

Chapter Three

NOAH Gunderson had traveled the world for years, soaking in everything he could in every culture he encountered along the way. He'd consumed yak butter tea in Nepal. Grappa in Tuscany. Ouzo in Greece. He even ingested boa constrictor in the Congo and *huitlacoche*, which is pretty disgusting corn fungus, in Mexico.

And now, it seems, he was about to swallow the bitter bile of rage, courtesy of one unfortunately hot-looking former love of his life, Harper Landry, right here in the confines of his Subaru Outback along the glorious coastline of North Carolina. Noah had hoped to avoid such an encounter by eventually approaching Harper on his terms, but fate had something entirely different in mind. Here he sat, temporarily driving Uber while he got his shit together, and there she perched, his fare for the next twenty minutes, with a date, no less. One whose hand—judging by the view when he readjusted his rearview mirror—was crawling up her thigh.

Well, fuck. This was so not the plan he'd mapped out in his head, which involved maybe lavishing her with flowers and champagne and perhaps even a puppy—she'd always wanted a puppy, hadn't she? But now, instead, not only was he about to get a well-deserved ream of steaming shit served on a silver platter, but he also had to digest the fact that he was delivering this evidently happy, horny couple to one address—and not hers, considering the unfamiliar locale. That meant she was likely heading to his house for a night of unbridled sex with this asshole who was staking his claim on the woman he'd fantasized about reconciling with after all these years (not to mention having bitter recriminations). Damn, he had his work cut out for him.

"Wait a minute—is that you, Harper?" He glanced in the rearview mirror in time to catch the lacerating glare of her eyes.

Her lip snarled. "Noah? Is that you? Noah love-'em-and-leave-'em Gunderson?" She threw him the stink-eye. "Not surprised you wouldn't recognize me. That usually happens when you leave without a backward glance."

Touché. He paused for a minute to collect his thoughts. He didn't want to blow it on the first go-round. He figured there were going to be many of these if he wanted to try to win her back. It wasn't going to be easy; even he recognized that he'd behaved like a cad when he left her with no warning. It was inexcusable, and he knew he'd better not start making excuses now.

Headlights coming toward him illuminated his passengers in the backseat. Glancing in his rearview mirror, he noted Harper had grown into a beautiful woman: those nearly translucent eyes he'd stared into so many times brought to mind the tropical waters of Bali. He'd spent time there and went on a whale watch in search of the magnificent blue whale, the largest animal on the planet, weighing in at 150 tons and up to 100 feet long. Truly a once-in-a-lifetime spectacle to behold. Yet as amazing as that was, was it better than the many quiet times he and

Harper spent holding hands, gazing into each other's eyes? Hard to say, but right now he'd give anything to have that back.

He stole a glance at her hair—it had the slightest glimmer of copper threading its way through the chestnut curls—and yearned to run his fingers through it again as he'd done so many times before. His fingers clutched the steering wheel as he gritted his teeth. He's the one who threw that all away. He wasn't entitled to be mad at her or even jealous of the doofus coming onto her in the back seat. Well, okay, he could be jealous of him. Pissed even. She was everything he remembered her to be, only instead of the ubiquitous smile boasting those bright white teeth, she wore a scowl that he knew was reserved for him. Talk about a sucker punch to the gut.

"I'm sorry I didn't let you know I was back in town."

"Huh," she said. "Why on earth would you? Seems entirely in keeping with your not letting me know you were leaving town. At any rate, you must've thought I'd want to know." She paused, her eyes thin slivers, like an angry snake. "You've obviously mistaken me for someone who cares."

She was always good at digging the knife in when she wanted to.

"I'm sorry. Of course not," he said, adjusting the rearview mirror again so he could get a better look at what that little shit was doing with Harper. He wasn't sure which was paining him more: her churlish rejection of him, or the fact that this man's hands were roaming her body while he had no other choice but to drive the car and feign ignorance.

God. Were they a couple? Had they been together for long? He'd received updates on Harper while his mother

14

was alive, at least until she was too sick to bother anymore. She'd adored Harper and had hoped so much that Noah would rethink things and try to reclaim his long-lost love. He felt awful that it took his mother's death to kick him hard enough in the ass to even attempt it. But maybe it was too late. He hadn't contemplated that and instead assumed that somewhere in the back of his selfish brain, she'd be waiting for him. That was his first mistake.

The car was silent but for the whoosh-whoosh of the windshield wipers and the thrum of raindrops on the car roof. Oh and the giggles emanating from Harper's mouth. Knowing that jerk was eliciting those responses from her was making Noah crazy. What was he doing? Where were his hands now? A glance in the mirror revealed him leaning toward Harper, his nose practically stuck in her ear. He was whispering sweet nothings, buttering her up, getting her ready for the close. Noah wasn't stupid. He was, after all, a guy and recognized the silent negotiations going on, the push-pull of who was going to be allowed to do what and when. Judging by the joyful noises coming from his ex-girlfriend, that dude was going to for gold. Four aces. A hat trick.

Crap. He couldn't let this happen right under his nose. Even if it was his own damned fault. He couldn't have finally figured things out in that obtuse brain of his, only to discover it was too late because this monkey was swinging from her tree while he chauffeured them around the greater Verity Beach metropolitan area. He needed to do something to thwart this. He realized he hadn't turned up his music again. Normally for a late-night call like this, he played seduction music; he figured the couple would appreciate the warm-up tunes. But now he switched to his world music channel, and the sound of a loud singer with a heavy synthetic drumbeat filled the car.

"So, Harps," he said. "I was under the impression you were single."

A look in the mirror revealed that diversionary question stopped Harper in her tracks. Sweet. Better still, it halted Mr. Wonderful from advancing the troops temporarily. For the win.

Harper frowned. "Do you mean now, or do you mean four years ago, when you left me high and dry while you indulged yourself and took off to sow your wild oats, or whatever the hell you were doing?"

Man, this was not going to be easy. Good thing Noah loved a challenge.

"About that." He arched his brow and flicked his turn signal on. The car was uncomfortably quiet save for the click, click, click of the blinker. The sound could've been his brain, trying desperately to come up with a good excuse. His mind was like a lighter that had run out of butane, so as many times as you might flick that flint, no flame was gonna start up. The sucky thing was he didn't have one.

Damn, life was so much simpler when you screwed up but had such an amazing explanation, the person you hurt couldn't remain mad. Shame he couldn't fabricate one right now. Fact was, he'd had four years to figure out the best way to explain it to Harper, and he'd not bothered to. Maybe in some ways, he hadn't delved deep enough into it. Maybe he'd been running so much he hadn't bothered with enough introspection. He knew he owed that to her. But how?

"I was hoping we could sit down and talk a little bit at some point in time?" He ended the sentence on an up-tone, attempting to be hopeful in the face of the undeniably pessimistic reality that she was more than likely about to go home and have sex with the douchebag next to her. "We've got a lot of catching up to do."

He ducked his head enough to catch her vigorously shaking her head in his mirror. "Oh, no," she said. "The only catching that was attempted was me trying to find you to figure out why you did what you did. Too little too late to try to make things nice now. My boyfriend and I are quite happy, thank you." To emphasize the point, she leaned in and kissed the bastard: her lips over his, mouth wide open. He clenched his jaw and squeezed hard on the steering wheel. It made him nuts to see her do that to such an undeserving character. Not that he knew a thing about him, but nevertheless that guy—and anyone after him—would always be the wrong man for Harper.

But what if the right guy had played his cards all wrong and blown it?

Chapter Four

HARPER used to wonder how she'd react if and when Noah came back. She'd rehearsed a hundred different responses, some of which might have involved a level of moderate yet uncharacteristic violence. For instance, there was that little fantasy about rewarding him for his betrayal with a solid left hook to his snout, which she could argue wasn't particularly mean under the circumstances; it would be practically well-deserved. It's not as if she'd thought about whipping out a stiletto blade and slicing his throat or anything. But then again, an appropriately placed kick with a stiletto *heel?* Well, maybe she hadn't quite ruled that out.

She wasn't one to hold grudges, but damn. Noah's near evaporation into thin air four years ago, only days after their college graduation, had left Harper desperate for answers she'd never have and so riddled with self-doubt that, well, she could barely figure out how to be in a relationship with another man if the opportunity arose. To date, it hadn't, and as a result, she hadn't truly faced her demons—she wasn't sure how she could ever trust a man again.

And then all of a sudden, right here, right now, the guy shows up? Talk about bad timing. She'd had a lovely evening with Danny Greevy and she'd enjoyed getting to know him a bit, until that was all eclipsed when, out of nowhere, Noah appeared and inserted himself into her little momentary happy bubble, sticking a sharp needle in to pop it. What the hell? Who died and gave him permission to do that to her?

On second thought, perhaps that wasn't delicately phrased, considering his mother had died not long ago. Or at least that's what Harper had heard through the grapevine. Even all these years later, people loved to keep her informed when someone had a bead on anything that might involve Noah.

Most often she politely explained that she no more wanted to hear about Noah than she wanted to be told she had an incurable disease. Usually that shut people up. Though plenty of folks had made certain she was aware that his mama had passed. Which was a shame—she thought highly of Millie Gunderson, who'd tried to stay in touch with Harper at first when her son pulled his runner. She'd sort of taken it personally herself, so Harper couldn't even be mad at her by extension. After all what mama would want her son to up and disappear like that? But still, it rankled Harper enough that she didn't want to deal with anything that had even the slightest DNA connection to Noah, so she quickly let slide that tenuous relationship. She stopped answering Millie's calls, and pretty soon Millie gave up reaching out altogether.

Harper always wondered if it was the legacy of Noah's father that drove him to skip town so unceremoniously. This was something Noah would never discuss, except to say that his dad had chosen early on to shun fatherhood— something about him being allergic to it. She figured if Noah ever wanted to discuss it, he would, so she let it be. *Allergic.* Perhaps it was more like there was a runaway gene that threaded through Noah's lineage, and he was only following the family mandate. Well, to hell with that. She had no obligation to be victimized yet again by that nonsense; she would simply avoid Noah Gunderson like the plague now that he was back in town. Driving Uber, of all things. Super weird since he was always planning to go to law school. Why on earth would he become a glorified cabbie instead?

She had even more unanswered questions about him, but she wasn't going to let that interfere with her lovely date. Danny was handsome and charming and thoughtful and funny, and she could show Noah what she thought about his dropping a precision-guided emotional bomb into her unwilling lap.

That's why she decided now was as good a time as any to make it abundantly clear where her allegiances lay—with the cute dirty blond whose thighs were pressed against hers in the backseat of her former boyfriend's car. Perhaps it was a little premature, but at least the message would be sent loud and clear: stay the hell out of my life, Noah Gunderson.

When she pressed her lips to Danny's, she presumed there would be the usual fireworks. Wasn't that always what happened when you kissed a guy? Inquiring minds wanted to know because to date, Harper's only experience with kissing a boy had been Noah. They'd dated all through middle and high school and even survived four years at Chapel Hill. He was her first—and last—kiss. After Noah, for a long time she'd had no interest. And then came everyone insisting it was time to get back on that horse, and with that came the succession of loser dates, and she sure as hell wasn't gonna waste the time and effort to swap spit with those guys. But she did assume that kissing led to the tingly feeling in your stomach, the swoony bit that made your head dizzy with excitement. When two peoples' lips locked, and their bodies were pressed to one another, the electricity that was generated... Wow. She'd completely given up on that after Noah.

Yet now here she was, just like riding a bike, only it felt a bit as if the bike had a flat tire. Maybe it took some working up to get to the good stuff.

As she released her lip-lock with Danny, she giggled, knowing it would make Noah crazy. Danny nuzzled her neck, and Harper caught Noah staring at the unfolding drama in the back seat with a look that was both pained and angry, his lips pinched but his eyes achingly sad. It almost made her feel bad for him.

"That was a pleasant surprise," Danny said, oblivious to the elephant that had plunked his ample ass smack dab in the middle of the car.

"Pleasant being the operative word," she said loud enough for Noah to hear. "That was quite nice."

"This is our stop," Danny said, coaxing his fingers through Harper's hair. "You still up for that nightcap?"

"Wouldn't dream of not coming in," Harper said, pasting on a hyperenthusiastic smile that she knew far exceeded her desire level. Sure, Danny seemed nice and all, but maybe this was going a little fast, and maybe she'd be better off going home. Better yet, maybe she'd be better off if Noah Gunderson had stayed the hell out of her life once and for all.

Chapter Five

NIGHTCAP? Noah grumbled quietly as he guided the car toward the curb in front of the cute little cedar shake beach bungalow that was the destination of his fare. One of whom was fair. The other of whom wasn't playing fair. Then again, what was that saying? All's fair in love and war? Doofus probably didn't even know there was a war going on. Doofus? More like Dean Martin, what with that cheesy "nightcap" line. Noah felt as if he was carting around part of the damned Rat Pack in the back seat.

Who even used the word nightcap? Maybe that guy who wrote "'Twas the Night Before Christmas," but that was written a couple hundred years ago, wasn't it? Then again maybe that was "kerchief," not a nightcap. Kerchief, nightcap, whatever. No matter the word, it was plain weird. What bozo lured women in with nightcaps in this day and age?

As Harper unfastened her seatbelt, Noah quickly stepped out of the car and scurried around to open her door for her, hoping the yahoo next to her would walk out the other door and keep on walking into the nearby ocean. It was high tide, after all. It wouldn't take long for him to fully submerge. A man could fantasize, couldn't he?

He reached a hand out to help Harper over a puddle

next to the curb. Surprisingly, she accepted it.

"Can I call you sometime, Harps?" Noah's eyebrows ski-sloped down toward the center of his face. God, he hated leaving her here to do whatever she might be about to do with this yutz. But what else could he do?

Harper shook her hand free of his and walked into the waiting arm of her dreary date. She turned her head toward Noah. "You've got to be joking."

With that, she followed the man up to his front door without a backward glance.

And Noah knew he deserved that.

Noah sat in front of the house for a few minutes longer, waiting to see which lights were turned on, and worse still, to see if any then were turned off, like a damned second-floor bedroom light. It killed him to imagine what might happen. That said, he didn't even want to think if they were too busy to bother flicking off the switch.

One thing was for sure: he was damn well turned on seeing Harper for the first time in so many years. He thought it impossible she could be even more gorgeous than before, but she was. Beautiful beyond words. Which only led him to question his own stupidity and cowardice all the more. Except that was water under the bridge at this point. You can't bring back yesterday, so why dwell on it? His mom always told him if you're busy looking back, you might miss what's ahead of you.

He decided it made more sense to focus on clues Harper had left behind. Little tiny verbal breadcrumbs scattered in the back seat of his car.

"Nice," he said, warming his hands in front of the car

heater. He'd turned off the AC, allowing his windows to steam up a bit. He hated that you had to keep it on even when the weather was cold. What a stupid design flaw that was, having to blast the heat with the AC on.

"Nice," he said, pressing his pointer finger to the condensation on the window and tracing the letters. N-I-C-E. "'Nice' works great if you're describing your favorite cousin Ginny. Or maybe a teacher you particularly liked in the third grade. As in, 'Oh, I thought Miss O'Grady was so nice!'" He laughed out loud at his dumb joke.

But nice? About a kiss? Hell no.

"Clue number two?" he said aloud. Then he drew the next word on the front windshield. "Pleasant." He underlined the word twice. "No woman who's horny and passionate for a guy says his kiss is 'pleasant.' You might say to your minister 'that was a most pleasant sermon.' Or you might discuss the temperature and say it was pleasant. But if a woman is hot for a man, pleasant is not in her vocabulary. At that point, she's not interested in talking. Rather she would be tugging up his shirt and grasping for his belt buckle and fumbling with the pants button so she could get her hands down there as soon as humanly possible." *Pleasant my ass.*

What this told him was that she was not serious with this wanker. One thing was clear: this was a first date. They obviously hadn't even kissed until she put on that little show for him. He was shocked she'd described it in such tepid terms. This was all good news. It gave Noah some breathing room, a chance to figure out a strategy to win Harper back.

Chapter Six

HARPER closed the door as quickly as possible behind her. She didn't want to risk Noah racing after her right into this man's house. She wouldn't put it past him. She looked up and made a quick assessment of the place. Cute. Bright, cheery, beachy, with blond wood furniture, aqua-and-white-striped lounge chairs, and a sunny-yellow sofa. Only at the beach could you get away with a sofa that looked like a giant lemon.

She would argue, though, that the décor in here fit far more with what a woman would choose than a man. But who knew? Maybe his sister decorated it for him. Or his mother. *Ugh, hope he isn't a mama's boy.* That would be bad. Oh, but it could be a rental, in which case who knew who decorated it? Maybe he bought it, lock, stock, and barrel. But a closer look showed it wasn't beat up enough to be a rental. No dings in the drywall. No scuffs on the hardwoods. The furniture looked like it came from that expensive home goods store on the beach road not far from her place. No one would buy nice things from there only to let renters beat the crap out of it.

"I've got a bar set up in the living room. And let me see if I can find the cat," Danny said. For a minute she was so lost in thought she'd forgotten about him. At least she was pondering home décor and not dirty, rotten ex-boyfriends who looked so damned handsome she wanted to scream. Ugh, Noah did look amazing, didn't he? Sort of rugged. The scruff of beard growth on his face looked delicious. And she didn't want to stare—at least not when he might have been looking—but when she'd glanced carefully in the rearview mirror, those almond-shaped hazel eyes she'd loved so much were reflected in it. His dark hair was shorter, but it still curled in wild waves at the nape of his neck. Which was someplace she used to love to bury her fingers; it felt like sinking your toes into a thick new carpet. "Any of those sound good to you?"

Oh crap. He said something she totally missed. She shook her head to erase those thoughts and instead smiled at him, devoting her full attention. "I'm sorry, I was so caught up in admiring your lovely home that I missed what you said."

He waved dismissively. "It's all good. I've got beer, wine, bourbon, tequila, Baileys, milk, orange juice. What sounds good?"

Harper scrunched her nose. "Definitely not milk. I mean maybe if you had some fresh-baked cookies. But then again, do you have some Kahlua? I could take a little of that with milk." She licked her lips and then wished she could unlick them—it felt too suggestive. Not that she hadn't already been Forward Franny with that kiss she planted on him in the car. Oy. What was she thinking? It was so outside of her personality to do that! Clearly she'd gotten rusty with so many years of neglect. She'd become the Tin Man of Sexual Inactivity. She didn't even know the proper protocol for kissing a near stranger. She blanched. Danny. Danny was actually a near stranger. Well, she'd spent several hours—enjoyable hours—with him tonight, but did she know him? For all she knew, he could be a serial killer and she wouldn't even realize it.

How awful would that be? After all this time, she finds a guy she thinks she could have some fun with and instead he ends up being like a psycho clown or something, one of those men who lures women with the promise of White Russians and beach views. Dressed in a clown costume, big red wig, blue-and-white polka-dotted one-piece get-up, large red shoes. And a gleaming butcher's knife.

Oh for goodness' sake: the man wasn't dressed in a clown costume. She was being ridiculous. He was a perfectly nice man offering her a drink. A nightcap, now that she thought of it. Which was such an odd thing to call it. So retro. No one said that word anymore, did they? Oh well, maybe he was old-fashioned that way.

Suddenly, she hoped he was old-fashioned in some other ways as well. *Please, dear God, don't have him jonesing to get into my pants tonight.* Upon further reflection, she didn't want her first sexual experience since Noah to be with a complete—or nearly so—stranger. Even if he did make a fine nightcap. She had to be a little bit more discerning than that. Although she'd been through a hell of a dry spell. Like Moses-and-the-Israelites-parched-in-the-desert dry spell. Which was crazy. How could it have been that long since she'd had sexual relations with a man? Relations. That was a weird one too. What did her mother sometimes call it? Sexual congress. Harper always pictured bald, paunchy men in the US Capitol gaveling in a meeting whenever she said that. Though for real, there were enough scandals in that place over the years, perhaps it was a fitting term.

Oh goodness. Her mind had taken to wandering like a lost child in the woods. This was not uncommon for Harper when she was frazzled. And she was frazzled.

Because she was unexpectedly hornier than a Cape buffalo, but she feared it wasn't the man before her who had stirred up a hornet's nest worth of buzzing in her nether regions. It was like that part of her had woken up from the damned dead upon seeing he-who-shall-not-be-thought-of for fear it might trigger some kind of spontaneous-combustion orgasm in her. She was a veritable sexual Rapunzel, dead to the world for ages and then *poof!* come and get it! Chuck wagon's ready! Although she certainly found use for her battery-operated "mystery date" several times a week, she'd pretty much had her legs clamped tight for far too long, and now all of a sudden, she was like a damned sexual volcano, about to burst right out of her lava chambers—if that's what you'd call it.

Breathe, Harper. Breathe.

She fanned her face, feeling desperately flustered.

"Sorry, can't seem to find the cat anywhere," Danny said, handing her a drink. It felt refreshingly cold, so she pressed it to her cheek. "You warm? I can open the sliding glass door." He walked over to the door, which led to a screened-in porch. She followed him.

"I know it's chilly outside, but I did get hot for some reason, so this would be great to cool down for a minute."

There was a breakfast table on the porch with two chairs and a porch swing, so she sat at the table to avoid having to figure out what she was supposed to do here. She was as nervous as a kid on the first day of school. Except this might end in flesh-to-flesh contact and the exchange of bodily fluids. Not quite the same.

She was grateful for the sound of crashing waves along the shoreline—it filled the conversational void she seemed incapable of pouring herself into.

"Bottoms up." Danny nodded and tipped his glass to

hers.

"Cheers," she said, taking a bit more of a swig than intended. She licked the residual Kahlua from her lips and nearly smacked herself for doing that. Again with the tongue action. "I'm sorry for that weirdly awkward scene in the Uber back there."

He sat down opposite her. "It's fine. I figured there must've been something there, but it's not my business."

She rubbed the bridge of her nose with her thumb and forefinger. "And about that boyfriend comment…" She made air quotes around the boyfriend. What a dingbat she was, claiming they were dating. Way to kill the chance of a second date.

He shook his head. "Again, I'm sure you had your reasons."

She nodded. "It sort of took me by surprise, is all. Suffice it to say I hadn't seen him in a long time."

He pointed his finger at her and then toward the door, as if Noah was still right on the other side of it, sitting in his car, waiting. "You two had a thing?"

She nodded, pursing her lips. "You could say that." She didn't want to get into the details. "Let's leave it at things ended badly."

He reached his hand across the table and rested it over hers. "I'm sorry, Harper. I can't imagine how someone would ever want to hurt you like that."

She heaved a sigh. Neither could she. That was the problem.

"It's complicated," she said. She took a look at her watch. It was late. The bloom was off the rose for this date tonight. To make matters worse, the cat wasn't even here. Maybe another night would be better. Under the circumstances, Harper couldn't see even having an innocent little make-out session with the guy. It would feel disingenuous. Not that she wasn't interested, but now her mind was polluted with too many thoughts: about seeing Noah again after all this time. About all that they'd been through together. About how he betrayed her. And about how crazy horny he made her feel even when he infuriated her, like he had right now. Damn him. Ruined everything by leaving and now he was ruining everything by showing up unannounced.

Part of her wanted to sleep with Danny and get it over with. Just be done with that thing looming over her head like a ghost. Oh, crap. Having sex with a cute date should never be viewed as an albatross. And it wasn't. She'd love to have sex with him. Or at least make out with him. Maybe some heavy petting. Heavy petting? She was starting to sound like a sex-ed class in middle school. What she meant was to have his hands on her private parts in a way that would make her feel the way she felt when Noah had done that.

She combed her fingers through her hair as she took another swig of her drink. Danny's fingers started to walk up her wrist, along her arm. She instinctually wanted to swat at his hand as if it was a mosquito. Ugh. That is not the proper response when an incredibly handsome, kind, eligible man is trying to show you he's interested in you.

Harper squeezed her eyes tightly. "No—I mean Danny. I know this is super lame of me, but I think I need to get back home. Can we maybe pick up where we left off another night? I had such a great time with you, but this sort of derailed me a little bit. I'd be much better company once I splash some water on my face, get a good night's sleep, and forget all about that whole car ride."

He frowned. "You sure?"

She nodded. "I'm sorry. We had such fun tonight. And I really would love to see you again."

He stood up. "Let me at least take you home."

She shook her head. "No. Please, I'm so good with taking an Uber back." She already had her phone on the table and opened the app to call for a ride. "No sense in your going back out in this weather."

"But I'm happy to."

She held up her hands in protest. "No, seriously. I insist. I will be fine. It's a quick ride home." She glanced at her phone. "See? Says my ride will be here in one minute."

She walked back into the house, took her drink to the sink, and poured the remainder down the drain, rinsing the cup and loading it into the dishwasher. She could at least be a considerate houseguest, albeit a fleeting one.

"Thank you, Danny, for such a lovely evening." She reached up and gave him a chaste peck on the cheek.

"Can I call you?"

She smiled. "Absolutely. I'd like that."

With that, she slipped outside into the driving rain, and to her chagrin, into the same damned Subaru Outback she'd exited less than an hour ago.

Chapter Seven

"ARE you fucking kidding me?" Harper said as she sat down in the back seat. It was obvious she had no intention of sitting next to Noah. "I should get out of this damned vehicle this minute. Except it's dumping out." She glared at him, hard. "Are you stalking me or something?"

Technically, no. But he had hung out in the same area in the hopes that she'd have a change of heart and leave before she did something foolish with that baboon. Not that she gave him any indication she'd do something so fortuitous for him. Based on her responses earlier, he'd almost have expected her to have a rousing round of revenge sex with the twit so she could throw it back at him.

"I can't exactly stalk you while I'm driving, can I?" he said. "I happened to be nearby. Not too many of us driving tonight. It's late and the weather sucks. I was the sole survivor I guess."

"Well, you're lucky it's such a stormy night, or I'd demand you let me out on the side of the road."

"In what universe would you ever expect me to allow that to happen, Harper?" he smiled into the mirror. He might have been a dick for leaving the way he did, but when they were together, he was the most attentive, considerate boyfriend going.

"To be honest, I don't know what to expect from you. Fact is, I used to expect something from you, and voilà, that was shot to hell in the blink of an eye. For all I know, you might choose to drop me on the side of the road. Wouldn't that be fitting?"

"Go on, Harps. Get it all out. Beat me up. I can take it. I deserve it. In fact, give me your best shot."

"You know what? I can give you a bad Uber rating." She punched the seat. "Then you won't bother me anymore."

"But you're not malicious."

"I could be if I wanted to be."

"Why would you want to be?"

"Because you're a jerk."

"Two wrongs don't make a right, Harper."

"Oh, so you admit you were wrong, then?"

He heaved a sigh. A quick glance at his GPS showed they were pulling up to her home.

"Your place?" He nodded toward a cute little gingerbread cottage tucked away on a less-developed stretch of Ocean Road. It appeared to be a new house, with other new homes in midconstruction all around her place.

"Yep," she said.

"Nice." He nodded. "Had it long?"

"Listen, Noah. I'm gonna be honest with you." She wiped her lips with her thumb and forefinger and reached for her purse, about to get out of the car. "There's no sense in small talk between the two of us. To be truthful, I've got zero fucks to give to you. And you've only got yourself to blame. You had the hammer and the bag of nails and you willfully pounded them right on into that coffin, destroying everything we had. So, sorry. Not sorry."

Noah frowned and opened his door.

"What are you doing?" she said as she opened her own door.

"I'm going to walk you up to your door like a gentleman."

He shut his door and took a step to catch up to her, placing his hand along the base of her spine, ushering her forward. She swatted at him. "I'm perfectly capable of walking to my own home, thanks."

"Look, Harper. I understand that you're angry with me. And you're entitled to be. But I have a responsibility to be sure that you get home safe and sound. So please, let me walk you to your door."

"I can assure you I've never had an Uber driver extend this service to me before, so I'm pretty sure it's not in the driver's handbook."

"Consider it a kind gesture from a friend."

She shook her head. "Dude, you gave up the opportunity to be my friend when you turned tail and ran without an explanation. So no. You and I"—she pointed at him and then at herself, shaking her head—"we're not friends. You're only someone I used to love."

She fumbled for her key, and it took long enough that he planted himself right up behind her as she pulled the fob out of her messy purse and slid the key in the deadbolt, giving it a turn. But it jammed instead.

"Dammit," she said, jiggling the thing to no avail.

Noah stood behind her, arms crossed, a sly smile on his face, trying not to look smug as she fought with the key. She frowned at him. "I think I can figure out how to work the key to my own house."

He shrugged. "Have at it."

She twisted and tugged on the key while more expletives erupted from those gorgeous lips of hers. God, he'd love to hear her saying those things while he was buried deep inside of her. He loved dirty talk and no one could talk dirty like Harper Landry. He could feel his pants growing tighter merely thinking about that.

At last he reached over and placed his hand on top of hers, calming her tense fingers, and he pressed the key a little deeper into the lock, then gave it an easy turn. "Sometimes you have to press in a little deeper." And yeah, he meant it both ways.

She shrieked at him in obvious frustration. "Goddammit, Noah."

He twisted the knob and opened the door, following so closely behind Harper she couldn't even slam the door on him, which he suspected she was inclined to do.

"Is that the thanks I get for ensuring you aren't stuck outside in the rain all night?" He was pressed up against her from behind, and could practically feel her body humming in response. He knew she wanted him as much as he wanted her.

"I don't owe you any thanks, Noah Gunderson. I owe you a swift kick in the—" Noah leaned over and nuzzled her neck, right in that spot she once loved so much. They used to joke that her Achilles heel was in her neck—the minute Noah got her there, she was putty in his hands. He placed soft kisses interspersed with the tiniest licks beneath her ear, and her breath came harder as he reached around and unbuttoned her coat, allowing him to slide his hands up over her breasts.

"This is not what I want," she said, but her hesitant response was as if she was turning down a decadent dessert because she'd decided to diet but didn't truly mean it. "Because I hate you, Noah."

Noah slid his hands to the V-neck edge of her dress,

deftly slipping his fingers beneath to the edge of her bra until he found her nipples and pinched them, hard. Harper moaned, loudly. It was the moan of a woman on the edge. He hoped for his sake it wasn't the edge of wanting to throttle him.

He groaned as he moved his lips up to her ear, swirling his tongue along the edge of it and inward. His cock had grown harder still in his pants, and he thrust softly against her ass, letting her know what she did to him. That she could arouse him in no time flat as if time hadn't passed since they last did this. He skirted one hand along her dress, tugging it up and sliding beneath the silky layers, following her thigh till he reached the lower edge of her panties. Slipping his fingers beneath, he savored her sharp intake of breath as she gasped when his fingers came in contact with her intimate flesh. He found her wet and warm center and stroked his fingers along her lips, like he'd done so many times, swirling her juices and then sliding first one finger, then another inside of her. Fuck, he wanted to be inside her so badly he was not going to last.

"Harper, baby, you're so slick and ready for me," he said as she moaned, thrusting her hips toward his questing fingers. He turned her around, swiftly removing her coat, pulling up her dress as he squatted down to his knees, too turned on to even notice the cold, hard tile of the foyer beneath them. He lifted one of her legs over his shoulder as his mouth found her pussy, and his tongue took long, slow passes along her seam before stroking around her clit.

"If you fucking stop now, I'll kill you," Harper said as she threaded her fingers through his hair, pressing his mouth to her core.

There was that dirty talk he was waiting for.

He looked up and her eyes were closed, her face

etched with pleasure. He picked up the pace of his fingers pumping into her wet channel as his tongue stroked her clit while she thrust into his face. "That's it, baby, rub your pussy on my face." She moaned and screamed out his name as she came hard, her body trembling with the effort.

"You'd better put that fucking cock into me before I kill you," she said, and he was perfectly happy to comply, quickly peeling his jeans down, then lifting Harper up and helping her wrap her legs around his hips as she settled herself onto his swollen cock.

"I hate you so much," Harper said. Only it wasn't her lips but her hips that were speaking the truth as they ground into Noah. He pressed his mouth to hers and they kissed like they had no choice, like the air would stop circulating and time would stand still and the earth would no longer rotate if they released their kiss. Harper pulled on his hair as her tongue dueled with his as if it was an epic battle she was determined to win. Noah gasped as he practically inhaled her mouth with his and then thrust his cock hard into her wet warmth, dismissing formalities, immediately quickening the pace, pumping faster and deeper. Finally he groaned and she moaned softly as he pressed deep inside of her and held her so hard to him he feared she'd end up with fingertip bruises on her hips. He came in hard jerks, and she quickly followed, her pussy clamping down on him as if it didn't want to let go. Their breaths came in clipped measures, and they heaved as sweat dripped from their brows.

"Oh my God, Harper." Noah paused to catch his breath. "That was intense."

He held tightly to her, not wanting to let go of the moment, the moment he'd dreamed of for so long when the two of them were joined again as one. But was this a one-off, or could this be the start of a newer, better phase of Harper and Noah?

Chapter Eight

HARPER wasn't sure which of the many mistakes she'd made was the worst of them. Could it have been giving damned Noah what he wanted, like she was someone he could swoop in and sleep with as if nothing had happened? Ugh, she was not happy with herself about that. But then again, she needed to give herself a hall pass for it: what girl wouldn't succumb, after not having any of that for so. damned. long?

Now, though, they'd done the deed. The man's penis had been inside of her duplicitous body moments ago, and she was nearly paralyzed with remorse—not because it wasn't incredible—it was as good as, if not better, than she remembered. But where on earth did she go from here? She was going to have to backpedal and let him know in no uncertain terms what just transpired was a big, fat, hairy mistake.

Which led her to the second problem: it was a big, fat, hairy mistake that could have quite negative consequences. She'd had unprotected sex with this guy. Granted the two of them had progressed past condoms long ago, but that was then, this was now. Lord knew where he'd had that thing since. Thank goodness she'd at least had the birth control component of things under control—she'd been on the pill for other reasons all along. But damn, when she thought earlier in the night about exchanging bodily fluids, she surely hadn't thought it was going to be hers and Noah's.

She hated the idea of having to have sex with Noah with a condom, though. Once you'd had skin on skin, it was no fun to deal with those unwanted barriers. And lordy, was it ever amazing. Talk about a long time coming. Literally.

Yet there were other flaws in her decision-making… For instance, the man lived here now. And she was likely going to run into him here and there, and now he would be that guy she had the one-nighter with, if you could call it that. More like impulse-control sex. And it was a hell of an impulse she couldn't control, dammit. She'd always been susceptible to Noah's charms, or pheromones or whatever it was that made her panties wet the minute she entered his sphere. But now she had to figure out how to get this man out of her home, her sanctuary, a place she didn't want tainted by memories of what could have been with Noah Gunderson.

"Sweetie, let's take this to the bedroom. My legs are about to give way," Noah said as he buried his nose in her hair.

Sweetie? Was he serious?

Harper quickly lowered her feet to the floor, the very tiled floor of her foyer that she apparently was incapable of getting past before having impulsive wham-bam-thank-you-ma'am sex with her ex. What the hell had she been thinking?

Of course. She hadn't been thinking. She'd been feeling. And that's what happened when you felt—you did stupid things like sex with Noah, and even though it felt a-

maz-ing, it was so not ever going to happen again. That man would never pass the threshold of her home if she had a say in it. She quickly tugged down her dress as she fumbled for her panties, which she found hooked on the doorknob. The doorknob. Oy.

"I'm sorry, but you need to leave." She couldn't even look him in the eyes.

He cocked his head and gave her a quizzical look.

"Leave? But—"

"But nothing, Noah. This was a huge mistake. I was gullible. It's been a long time since I did that. I only did it to relieve pressure. Sometimes a girl needs to have a good orgasm. I was simply using you to end my dry spell. The garden needed watering since it was awfully parched. It has nothing to do with me wanting you. Just so you know."

Noah nodded. "Ah. I see. So you didn't sleep with that loser you were with tonight? That's good to know."

Harper's eyes grew wide. "Loser? *Loser?* I'm sorry, you want to discuss losers? How about instead we can talk about Danny, who's a good guy and sweet and thoughtful and has an awesome sense of humor and he shows up for dates and he's respectful and I'm sure he'd never walk away from someone without even a word. Trust me, next time I am indeed going to sleep with Danny Greevy, not that it's any of your business. But if you do anything to get in the way of my having the most amazing sex on the planet with him, well, well, well, you'll have me to answer to."

Noah pulled up his pants, placed his hands on either side of Harper's face, then settled his lips over hers in a soft, gentle kiss that she had no choice but to go along with despite herself.

"Keep telling yourself that, Harper." With that, he turned and opened the door, stepping into the cold rain.

Only this time, he did turn around and looked right into her eyes as he walked backward to his car. "Keep telling yourself that."

Chapter Nine

NOAH sat in his car in front of Harper's place for a good long while. Resting his forehead on the top rim of the steering wheel, he wrapped his arms around either side of it, lost in contemplation. He couldn't believe what had actually happened. Never in a million years would he have expected to run into Harper, let alone have sex with her. But damn, thank goodness for tender mercies.

Sure, after the fact, Harper had demonstrated some buyer's remorse. But that was to be expected, regardless of when and if they had ended up sleeping together. Inevitably she was going to have to reconcile with a lot of things concerning Noah's actions if there was any chance of somehow getting back together. He understood that. But what he hadn't expected was how powerful this experience would be. At that moment when he was deep inside her and they both came, it was downright spiritual. He wasn't going to admit it to a soul, but a tear even trickled from the corner of his eye. And he couldn't admit that he wasn't as freaked out as he should have been when he failed to think of using a condom.

Part of the intense feelings came from realizing how loaded it all was for the both of them emotionally. He couldn't blame her one bit for hating him. He knew he'd been a coward to up and leave as he did. Being young and scared wasn't an excuse, and he needed to own it.

But when he'd found out his brother Matthew got a girl pregnant, it had spooked the hell out of him. Sure, he and Harper had talked about a future together back then, but it was off in the distance still, and it was almost like make-believe, not real. Shit got totally real the minute Matthew had to face the reality of being a father at the age of twenty. He hadn't even finished college yet, and suddenly he was forced to make lifelong plans when he didn't even know what his plans would be in a year. This with a young woman he'd only been dating casually.

That was all it took. Noah counted up the money he'd been saving over the years, bought a backpack and some hiking boots, secured the cheapest overseas plane ticket he could find, threw his passport in his back pocket, and that was the start of his big adventure. In total, two glorious years roaming the world, picking up occasional odd jobs along the way to help keep afloat financially, bartering his time for room and board whenever possible. He'd traveled to six continents before returning to the States to attend the law school he'd deferred acceptance to. Until his mother got sick and he realized he hated law school and was only doing it because he felt as if he needed to do something legitimate in the world. So he returned to Verity Beach, held his mother's hand as she fought the cancer that ravaged her body, and tearfully bid her a heartbroken farewell.

Now he found himself picking up the pieces of her financially mismanaged life, after having promised her that he'd ensure her quaint beachfront inn would not fall into the hands of creditors. That meant long hours poring through her books and tax returns trying to make sense of the fiscal mess she'd left behind, followed by late nights of driving Uber, because he needed a reliable source of income at least for the time being. And the income had been fantastic throughout the busy summer season and well into the autumn wedding season. Even now as cold weather was setting in, there were plenty of locals who relied on Uber for their social lives—it sure beat worrying about alcohol consumption while out at dinner or a party.

He'd been back for several months, biding his time before attempting to reach out to Harper. For one thing, he'd been tied up with his mother's illness until recently. In addition, he expected he'd get a frosty reception at best, and who knew how bad at worst? Hell hath no fury and all that. He wanted to be prepared for every eventuality.

Besides, he still hadn't figured out how to explain to Harper why he did what he did. Especially since there was no good reason. At least to her way of seeing things; he understood that. So instead he'd been spinning his wheels, waiting for the ideal moment. Who'd have known fate would drop her in his lap like that.

But now he had to focus on the best way to win back the woman he now realized had always been the love of his life. And what just happened between the two of them merely cemented the deal.

Operation Woo Harper Landry was on.

Harper lay in the dark, revisiting what had happened over and over in her mind. That Noah showed up out of nowhere blew her away to begin with. But then, she didn't even confront him and instead answered the siren call of what were clearly overactive hormones on her part? After all she'd been through? Hell, it had taken her two years to finally let go of him. Two years with no calls, no messages. Not even a damned postcard.

She'd heard through the rumor mills that he was off wandering the world, or sowing his wild oats, or whatever it was that stupid males did when they disappeared. She tried to avoid any information or updates on Noah. Each time she'd heard of his escapades, it picked open the sore and caused more pain. Eventually people understood that Noah was a subject not to be raised. So perhaps even if people had heard, she'd never know.

Her best friend, Allie Ledbetter, would have been on the phone with her no matter if it was the middle of the night had she gotten wind of Noah's presence. But Allie had been out of the country for months, living in Italy, so she didn't hear of these things quickly enough. Shame, as this time, Harper would have loved some advance warning about Noah's return. That way she could have at least locked down her damned chastity belt a little tighter. Instead she'd practically oiled up the lock and handed the man the damned key!

She'd seen the hint of a tear in his eyes when she couldn't pull her gaze away from his while he was buried deep inside her. It almost made her feel sorry for him. Almost. But then it sucker punched her back to reality. Those were crocodile tears, as far as she was concerned. He did this to himself—not to mention to her—and he wasn't entitled to cry. Even if it did make him seem vulnerable and loving.

Luckily she recovered quickly and let him know in no uncertain terms that what had transpired was merely sex.

Nothing else. And the only reason she allowed him down her pants—or up her dress, more accurately—was that she had an itch that needed some serious scratching. And God, was he good at that sort of scratching.

She closed her eyes and pictured him. Perhaps it was for the better that she hadn't even seen all of him naked. It was more than enough to look into those eyes of his and remember, despite his actions, the intense love she'd felt for him for so many years. The cocky smile he had, one side of his mouth a little more upturned than the other, with those irresistible dimples sealed the deal. He wasn't a boy anymore—he'd filled out and become all man. Even his face, with that scruffy beard... the last time she'd pressed her face to his, he was only shaving every couple of days.

She could barely admit it to herself, but she wanted him again. Already. Despite everything. She'd gotten a taste of what she'd once had, and while it made her all the more angry that he'd taken it away from her, she couldn't help fixating on some way—any way—she might have another chance to feel his body pressed to hers. As long as she made sure that this time her heart was not going to be in jeopardy. So maybe she'd give him a taste of his own medicine, reel him in while having her needs met a little bit. Servicing Harper was the least he could do after everything he'd done to her.

Chapter Ten

HARPER woke up agitated. Thank goodness she didn't have to work today. Or maybe that would have been better—keeping busy was preferable to staying home alone dwelling on the events of the night before, which still seemed like some weird dream. An incredibly sexy dream that left her body buzzing with need for more of where that came from.

She wanted to know more about how Noah got back here, but she didn't want to ask just anyone. Heaven forbid it got back to him that she was asking around. No way. She had far too much pride for that. She picked up the phone and called her best friend.

Allie had gone to Italy for the wine harvest, with the intention of returning as soon as it was completed but in the meantime had fallen in love with some handsome Tuscan wine baron or something. She had decided to take a little sabbatical and see how her relationship unfolded, which meant that the two best friends were relegated to long-distance communications. It had been bad enough when Allie was working clear across the country in Calforina. While Harper had been looking forward to her friend returning to their hometown, maybe it wasn't such a bad thing, since now Allie would now be forever preoccupied with her man first. Now she had one less girlfriend to occupy her time with even if she'd come back here with him.

The phone rang several times before her friend picked up.

"Ciao, bellissima."

"Oooh, your accent sounds even better since the last time we spoke," Harper said.

"I have the perfect teacher." Her friend laughed.

"Yeah, I know all about the Italian your boyfriend is teaching you. Most of which is unprintable."

"Oh, but trust me, it sounds amazing when you're in the heat of passion."

"You're going to rub this in that you're having passion and I'm not?"

"I'm sorry, Harps. If you come visit me, I'll see if Francesco can find another gorgeous Italian man for you. I swear to you, they are practically a dime a dozen around here."

"Believe me, I'd love to take you up on your offer. But I've got some pressing concerns I need to talk to you about. Although you are sworn to secrecy. You hear me?"

"Whoa! Cryptic. You've got me so intrigued now."

"You promise you won't breathe a word to a soul?"

"Harper, even if I did, it would be translationally polluted—my Italian is not that good. The only ones I'd even be able to tell would be Francesco and his family. And it would probably come out all wrong anyhow. Suffice it to say my Italian needs a little work."

"Except when it comes to discussions about what one does with body parts in Italian."

"Yeah, that."

"But I don't want you going onto Facebook and telling

any mutual friends. Don't call your cousin Franny who we all know has the loudest mouth on the planet."

"I haven't talked to Franny in over a year."

"I'm only saying, this is cone of silence stuff I'm about to divulge. You crossing your heart?"

"Done. Now spill. And please don't tell me you're pregnant. Last I heard you had been on a succession of dates with loser dudes that I know you'd never sleep with anyhow."

Harper rolled her eyes. Pregnant. Did she even dare tell her how stupid she was on top of how stupid she was, what with the going bareback? She heaved a sigh. "The good news is no, there is no pregnancy. And theoretically won't be, because thank God I'm on the Pill."

"Wait a minute. Are you telling me you had sex—like real, live actual penetration? With a man? One who has a penis?" Harper could hear her squealing with joy in the background. "Oh my God. Harper. Finally! I knew you'd find someone you'd want to have sex with again someday. I mean, I didn't think it would take this long and all. And to be truthful, I wish you'd have just fucked someone— anyone—to get it over with. If you had, it would have been much sooner. But I understand, sometimes some of us are late bloomers. And I guess whatever you'd had with he-who-shall-not-be-named was somehow especially precious to you. And I get it. I mean we all loved Noah. And who knows why he lost his shit the way he did. As much as I hated him for that, I never thought he meant to hurt you. Oh God, I'm on pins and needles. Do I know who it is you finally—*finally!*—slept with?"

"You are seriously harshing my buzz here, Allie. Because when I do tell you, you're going to then freak on me and that's going to freak me out more and ugh—" She took a sip of coffee that turned cold in her mug while she'd ruminated for the past hour.

"You didn't sleep with like our high school principal or something, did you?"

Harper did a spit take with her drink, spraying coffee all over the breakfast-room table. "No, I didn't hook up with Mr. Harbinger."

"That's a relief. I mean, he's sort of old. And married. And old."

"And married."

"It's not someone too young, is it? That would be kind of icky."

"Oh, this one is, sadly, entirely age appropriate." Harper pinched the bridge of her nose. What the hell had she done? Maybe she shouldn't be sharing this with Allie. But she needed to talk to someone, and at least that person was her best friend, conveniently far from home and less likely to spread the word. Or meddle. Knowing Allie, she'd try to push the two of them back together. She was a big fan of happy endings. So was Harper until she got the old heave-ho and missed out on hers. "Age appropriate, but life inappropriate."

"Would you say it already?"

"Okay, on the count of three. One." Harper took a deep breath. In through the mouth, out through the nose. "Two." She closed her eyes. *Pretend you're getting a shot. Clench your teeth, squint hard, and it'll all be done.* "Three. Okay, I slept with Noah Gunderson."

The line was silent.

"Allie?"

"Yeah. I'm here," Allie said. "Look, honey. We've been friends forever. I know you slept with Noah. I mean I slept with Jimmy Cusack back in high school. We all did.

Why are you telling me this now?"

"Gah! Allie! I mean I slept with Noah. Last night."

"Omigod, omigod, omigod. Shut the eff up. You so did not. What? How?"

"How? How do you sleep with someone? It usually means that you let his penis enter your vagina—"

"I know that! I mean how? Where? When? What? Huh?"

Harper heaved yet another hard sigh.

"Evidently Noah's back. I mean actually, he's back. And I went on a date—"

"You and Noah had a date?"

"No! I had a date with a guy. An honest-to-goodness sweet guy who I hope to date more. And then I slept with Noah."

"There is so much more that must have happened in between all of that. Start from the beginning, please."

"Right. So I had a date. For once the guy was really sweet. We had a great time. I decided I'd go back to his place for a drink. I call up an Uber, and who is my Uber driver but Noah. In a Subaru Outback, of all the damned things."

"Noah's driving Uber? I thought he was wandering the world. Or in law school. Or something like that."

"Law school?"

"Honey, remember? I swore long ago I'd not keep you up to date on your ex."

"Good point."

"So why is he back home?"

"Hell if I know."

"You slept with him and didn't even ask that?"

"Honestly not a lot of words were exchanged."

"No words were exchanged?"

"Not many. But plenty of body fluids."

"Harper, you're killing me here. Talk."

"Fine. I was trying to, but you kept interrupting me. So Noah dropped us off at Danny's place—"

"Sort of awkward."

"Completely. Not to mention buzzkillish. I mean here I was giving myself a pep talk that I could even sleep with this guy—"

"Which guy?"

"My date!"

"Okay, so you're about to have sex with this Danny guy, and instead you have sex with Noah when?"

"So I finally bailed on Danny. It was rainy, yucky, so I called for another Uber. And lo and behold, Noah shows up as my driver again."

"And you do it in his car?"

"No! I'm not that tacky."

"I think that would be kind of fun."

"Yes, it would be fun. But I mean not under the circumstances. He shows up in town and bam, I bang him in his car?"

"Well, then where did you?"

"First of all, it was the last thing in my plans."

"Always is."

"What do you mean?"

"I mean no one ever means to have sex with an ex-boyfriend. Especially one who broke your heart."

"You can say that again."

"Except it happens anyhow."

"You can say that again also."

"Please continue."

"Oh yeah, right. So I'm getting out of his car, he walks me to my door, my key gets jammed in the lock, he helps get it out, I have one foot in the foyer, and the next thing you know I'm up against the wall with my dress up to here and his pants down to there."

"Oh God, Harper, that sounds so passionate."

"That's one word for it. I might call it foolish. Or irresponsible. Or impulsive."

"Or horny."

"That too."

"But it's so exciting! You did it! You're over your dry spell! Albeit with the last man on the planet I'd expect that from, but hey, sometimes you gotta take what you can get in life. Or in your case what you're willing to give. You could've gotten it from many men, but you didn't."

"Yeah, but Allie, now I've had sex with my enemy."

"You could view him more as your frenemy. Or lovermy," she clucked out loud. "Nah, that sounds weird."

"Either way, I should never have done that and worse still, dammit, I want to do it so badly again that it almost makes my mouth water."

"So then do it again."

Harper's eyes grew wide. "Are you crazy? Once was impulsive. Twice would be sheer stupidity."

"Or you could call it practice."

Harper laughed. "Practice for getting my heart hurt again?"

"You're not going to let that happen—I'm sure of it. And quite frankly my guess is that he has no such intentions. It's interesting, though, that you didn't even know he was back. And the fact that he's driving Uber means he's working at home, which means he must be living back in Verity Beach. So I wonder what brought him back. And how long it's been. And why he didn't reach out to you—except that he feared you'd lop off his balls, maybe—and wow, what kismet that he ended up being your driver. Kind of like your knight in shining armor. Only in a Subaru Outback."

Harper groaned. "I'd think that would be funnier if it wasn't so unfunny, you know."

"Oh, this is actually so very entertaining. I am quite excited to watch this unfold from afar. I can't wait to hear what happens next."

"Are you suggesting there should be a next?"

"I'm saying there damn well better be because I want to hear every little bit about it."

"Trust me, the only thing that might happen is me taking advantage of the proximity of his very familiar penis."

"Which was as good as ever, I presume?"

Harper let out a little moan. "Better, unfortunately."

She could hear her friend clapping in the background. "Oh, Harper. Hurray. Yes, yes, you need to take as much advantage of that thing as possible. And keep me posted on your progress."

"For that matter, the only progress that might happen is I might be able to catch up on some long-lost sexual satisfaction."

"Baby steps, my dear. Baby steps."

Baby steps, indeed. Harper resolved to make room for some Harper time. And if getting with Noah helped in that regard, well, then, it would have to suffice. Maybe she'd simply suffer through sex with Noah for the cause.

Chapter Eleven

NOAH had been promising his brother he'd babysit for his nephew for months now, and Matthew had cashed in at last.

"Dude, thanks for taking Tyler for the night," Matt said as he handed a list of childcare instructions that looked more like a book manuscript it was so long and involved.

Noah held the multipage, stapled document aloft, dramatically leafing through the pages. "Is there a character arc in this? Obviously Tyler's our protagonist, but who's the antagonist?"

Matt grinned. "You, naturally."

"I would argue that as the parent you'd be the obvious foil for our hero."

"Yeah, but I'm the one who saves him from any and all disasters," Matt's wife Katie said, leaning in to kiss her brother-in-law hello on the cheek. "And if there are any disasters that befall him while we're out to dinner, you have me to answer to." She aimed her thumb at her chest. "And I can be a mean sonofabitch when it comes to my son."

Noah patted Katie on the back. "Rest assured, the only danger that could befall Tyler might be a bit of a sugar buzz." He pointed to a Ziploc bag he'd set on the counter. "Chocolate-chip cookies. Made them myself."

Katie smiled. "I know you were an absentee uncle for a long time, and you're doing a fine job of making up for lost time. But consider yourself warned: kids and sugar at bedtime is never a good combination."

He shrugged. "Yeah, I might well live to regret it, but the good news is I get to go home and have a good night's sleep either way."

She jokingly punched him on the arm. "And Matt and I might just decide to find a hotel room for the night and leave you to your own devices. Now play nicely, you two." She pointed to her little boy, who had a mess of spaghetti sauce smeared all over his mouth and random noodles strewn around the table and on his lap. "And Uncle Noah's going to give you a nice, warm bath before bedtime, so you're shiny and clean. Love you, baby doll!" She gave her son a bunch of kisses all over his face, wiped the sauce she picked up off her own face, and they waved goodbye.

Noah sat down next to his nephew. "So, kiddo. You're doing a bang-up job of that meal. You care to share any with your super hungry uncle?"

"No fork," the boy said.

"No problem," Noah said. "That's what we have hands for." He reached over and scooped up pasta with his fingers and shoved it into his mouth. The child giggled.

"Mommy says no hands," he said. But he dropped his fork on the ground and didn't bother to pick it up, instead grabbing a small fistful of noodles and forcing them into his mouth.

Noah chewed his noodles then opened his mouth wide. "Say ah!"

Tyler belly laughed hard, and it reminded Tyler what a prick he was not being there for this adorable little boy for all those years.

Of course his nephew mimicked him, and they both made nom-nom sounds as they ate like cavemen for the rest of the meal.

After they'd finished, Noah took a look at the table and floor beneath them. "Gah!" he said. "Uncle Noah is a pig!" He made oinking sounds and pushed his nose up, and the boy joined in the fun until he fell into Noah's lap laughing.

"What say we get this cleaned up and then we go right to dessert?" He lifted his brow. "There's cookies and ice cream in your future if you'll help me."

The two carried their dishes to the kitchen, and Noah gave Tyler a sponge to ostensibly wipe up after himself. It worked about as well as he expected, but he figured it was good training so let it go at that.

He grabbed the ice cream from the freezer and filled two bowls, topping each one with a cookie. "Oh," he said, holding up a finger. "I almost forgot." He walked toward the refrigerator, opening the door and pulling out a can of whipped cream. He swirled it on top of each cookie to the boy's wide-eyed joy.

"More!" he said.

"More whipped cream?"

"Yes!" He nodded his head vigorously.

"Ahhh… I've got an idea." He leaned over his nephew, aiming the whipped cream at his chin, making a little beard, then finishing it off with a fake mustache. He then repeated it on himself. He grabbed Tyler's hand and raced with him to the bathroom so they could have a look in the mirror, where Tyler clapped in delight. "I tell you what—let's preserve this for the books." He grabbed his phone and snapped a picture of the two with their whipped cream facial hair, then took a big lick of his nephew's chin, whereupon Tyler did the same back to him. They quickly licked their faces clean in between more selfies, returning to dig into their main dessert.

"I want you to babysit every day!"

Noah laughed. "I have a sneaking suspicion your mother might feel differently after she sees these pictures."

After they cleaned up their dessert mess, Noah ran a bath and helped Tyler into the warm bubbles. He splashed and played and got Noah sufficiently wet, and soon the bubbles dissipated and the water grew tepid. Which was when the child decided it was time to play with his penis.

"I guess they start 'em young with the right equipment." Noah laughed. "Remember, grasshopper, that thing will be your best friend, so treat him well. And while you're at it, use that only as a tool for good in the world. You rope a girl in with that thing, you fall in love, then don't go doing stupid things you'll regret, you hear?"

Tyler kept diddling his private parts, totally tuning Noah out.

"You know, your father was far more honorable than I was. And I wasn't even the one with the huge life-changing news. Damn. He was the one who had to rethink everything. And yet there I was, happy in a relationship, but I got so damned scared, I ran. What a wanker."

Tyler giggled. "Wankuh."

Noah nodded. "Yeah. That." He pulled the plug from the drain and plucked the child from the tub, wrapping him tightly in a soft towel.

"You ready for a couple of bedtime stories, my little man?"

Tyler nodded and ran naked toward his bedroom, his uncle in hot pursuit.

Chapter Twelve

FOR all these years, Harper had managed to avoid even attempting to spy on Noah on Facebook. She didn't even know if he was on there. It didn't matter. She didn't want to know about him, about his life, whether he was married or dead or had joined a cult. It was much, much easier to pretend he didn't exist.

But now, dammit, she could not eradicate thoughts of Noah from her brain. She almost felt like that stupid schoolgirl who was waiting for the high school quarterback to call after the one time he glanced her way. Only she hadn't even given Noah her number. And she'd made it clear she was off-limits. And she didn't know if she never wanted to see him again or wanted a command performance, stat. Though she was afraid the latter was what she was after. Crap.

She was sitting at the bar in her kitchen. She'd poured a tall glass of wine, closed her eyes, took a deep breath, and opened her laptop. She clicked on the favorites bar and opened up to Facebook, the giant time suck that seemingly swallowed human beings whole, never to be seen again. Sadly Facebook seemed ready-made for a girl who was home alone on a Saturday night. A girl who'd yet to hear from the man she should have been pining for a little more than for the untrustworthy ghost from her past.

She was a little disappointed that Danny hadn't even sent her a text, but then again, who knew how these things were supposed to unfold? Maybe she should be glad he didn't view her as an insta-booty call. Maybe it was respectful that he was allowing some time before reaching out to her. *Some time.* It had been a full week. That was kind of like an epoch when it came to dating. Or at least it should be. She could have even called him but she was simply not that girl. It would have felt a little forced to glom onto him like that.

The screen opened onto her homepage, and she scrolled up to the top bar and typed in Noah's name. Immediately a link popped up, and she clicked on it. Phew. He had it set so that everyone could see his posts, which would make her subterfuge imminently more achievable.

She was about to look through his photos but was instantly drawn in by the first one she saw: Noah and a child, their faces covered with shaving cream or something. They were both smiling in the selfie. The next one showed Noah licking the child's face. Obviously not shaving cream. Must be whipped cream. But who was this child? He looked to be about three or four years old. Wait. Three or four. *Oh my God. That's why Noah left me! He got some other girl pregnant! Clearly while we were together. Oh God, oh God, oh God. He was fooling around on me even before he left? And I thought we were so happy. What a bastard. What a dirty, rotten bastard. It was bad enough he left me, but now I know why and honestly, I could kill the man.*

It was too late to call anyone, so she typed a message to Allie.

SOS. Go check out Noah's Facebook page. You're not gonna believe it. He's a freaking baby daddy.

She couldn't bear to look at any more of Noah's alternate life. The one that could and should have been hers, had he not betrayed her even more than she'd realized. She shut her laptop and rested her head on the countertop as tears filled her eyes.

Everything had seemed so perfectly normal that final day they spent together. Harper and Noah had gone to dinner at their favorite restaurant; then they walked along the boardwalk. Afterward, they went out to a small private beach that only the locals knew about and spread out a blanket between the sand dunes, which hid them from anyone who might also show up at the beach. They'd made love beneath a blanket of stars, brilliant pinpoints of light that seemed like beacons calling them into the stratosphere.

Afterward, they lay curled up together, talking about the usual things: Noah's departure for law school later in the summer and how Harper was reluctant to leave Verity Beach, even though she'd likely have to move to the Raleigh-Durham area to get a better job.

"I wish you weren't going to be so far away," she said, swirling her finger along his chest as she talked quietly. He was planning to attend school in Washington, DC, which meant long road trips.

"Let's not think about that right now," he said. "Who knows what could happen between now and then."

In hindsight, those words were a bellwether, but at the time she thought nothing of it.

The next day, Harper texted Noah to see if he wanted

to go for a run on the beach. He said he had something he had to do, so she ran without him. She called him later in the afternoon to see if he wanted to do something, and she got his voicemail. A few hours later she called again, and nothing. Finally she went to his house, pounded on the door over and over, but no one answered. By then she had gotten scared—she even called the police to be sure there hadn't been an accident.

The next morning she found a letter in the mailbox with her name on it. She ripped open the envelope to find a cryptic letter with no explanation.

Dear Harper,

I know this will come as a shock to you, and I'm really sorry. I can't explain things right now, but I want you to know that I've decided to get away for a while. I needed to figure a lot of things out. I hope you'll understand, and even more so I hope someday you'll forgive me. Please know I'm not doing this because of you, but because of me.

I love you,

Me

Harper couldn't begin to count the number of times she read and reread that letter those first few months after Noah ran away, trying to find some stupid clue about why he left the way he did. It was like trying to divine tea leaves—futile yet impossible to stop trying. She tried to grill his mother to no avail. She was equally clueless about it and likely even more upset. It was hard to explain to her family and friends how deeply the betrayal affected her—it was visceral, to the gut. Sure he said it wasn't about her, but that's ridiculous. It *had* to be about her. Otherwise he'd never have left. There was something about her that wasn't worth sticking around for. And the worst thing was, she had no freaking idea what that could be.

Chapter Thirteen

NOAH was beat. He'd been up since early prepping the Smuggler's Inn for a wedding that would be held there this weekend. He hadn't made it to bed till almost three in the morning after picking up fare after fare. There had been a concert in the huge outdoor amphitheater about twenty-five minutes away, so he made some good money at least.

He wasn't up for getting together with a surfer friend he'd made, Spencer Willoughby, for drinks as promised weeks earlier when it had sounded like such a great idea. By now most of the friends Noah had grown up with had moved elsewhere. He was kind of lonely, so he wanted to connect with either other friends or new people. Matt had Katie—and Tyler, that cute little nug who'd stolen his uncle's heart instantly. His mom was gone. He was alone at the inn except for two sweet retired ladies who helped with the cooking and cleaning. And his lifestyle didn't lend itself to meeting new people much. Unless you counted the transient guests who stayed at the inn.

Things were starting to feel dire. Maybe he was going to have to sign up for one of those online dating sites. Although he knew deep down he wasn't going to do that. There was only one person he wanted to date: a green-eyed girl whose heart he inadvertently broke on the way to finding his way in life. The woman who was now collateral damage in his journey to self-discovery, which seemed so damned mercenary. He wished he'd gotten Harper's number; he wanted so much to talk to her. Granted he knew where she lived now, but he also didn't want to stalk her—that would be particularly creepy. He needed to let things unfold organically. She knew he was here now. She knew that in no uncertain terms he was back. And wanted her, desperately so. In some ways, the ball was now in her court, yet it killed him that maybe she had no intention of picking up that ball and running with it.

He checked the clock on the dashboard of his car: he had a good twenty minutes until Spencer would be here. He might as well go in and sit at the bar, catch up on sports highlights. Beat sitting in a cold car, especially now that it was getting dark so early. Winter seemed like it was looming with shorter days and chilly nights.

He entered the martini bar—weird place for two dudes to meet up, he thought—and lumbered over to the leathered granite bar. It was early enough that not many people were there yet. A cluster of three young women sat at the far end of the bar, heads together in conversation. Then he noticed a familiar tumble of chestnut hair, several seats away. Attached to a luscious body with a form-fitting baby pink fuzzy sweater. Sitting alone at the bar.

He tried to maintain his cool as he wandered toward her and pulled up a barstool. "I wish I could think of a clever pickup line, but all that is coming to my head is offering you a nightcap." He grinned.

She rolled her eyes. "Honestly, Noah. Did you attach some kind of homing device to me? Maybe a GPS tracker in my purse?"

"If only I'd thought of that. But I'll take that under

advisement." He winked. "Mind if I sit down?"

She glanced at the chair he'd already parked himself on. "Looks as if that's a moot point."

"Yeah, well, I'm hoping you don't call the bouncer to evict me." He glanced around. "Although this place is too high end to have a bouncer." He tapped the bar to motion to the bartender, then turned to Harper. "So tell me. What's a nice girl like you doing in a place like this?"

"And you thought nightcap was cliché?" She took a slip of her cosmo. "If you must know, I'm meeting Danny here for drinks."

"Danny, eh? I knew a guy once in kindergarten named Danny. He ate flies."

She pursed her lips in a pout. "Ha. Ha. So funny I forgot to laugh."

"You sure you want to meet up with this guy? It could be the very same fly-eating marauder from my childhood days."

She tipped her head down and threw him a look. "You're forgetting that you and I were in kindergarten together, Noah. That was Danny Finkelstein. He's a professional chef now."

Noah clapped at the irony. "That's wonderful," he said. "His discerning palate was evident at an early age."

He glanced over at the entryway as he saw the door opening. Dammit. Mr. Wonderful, Nightcap Danny, was heading their way, but then he diverted toward the restrooms.

"Hey, listen, uh, Harper. I was hoping you'd share your number with me. Maybe sometime we could get together and talk."

She lifted her brow. "I think we're all talked out, don't you?"

He shook his head. "Oh baby, you haven't yet seen the type of conversation I'm capable of."

"Really? Noah? Can't we let it all go?"

"You mean what happened between us last week didn't affect you the same way it affected me?" And boy had it affected him. He'd had to rub one out twice a day since then.

"I don't want to talk about it."

"You don't want to talk about it? Or you don't want to talk?"

She pursed her lips. "Neither."

"Aha!" he said, punctuating the air with his pointer finger. "So that means it did affect you. Can I be honest with you?"

"Something tells me you're going to be one way or another."

"I'm getting hard thinking about it. You?"

"Uh, no, I can assure you I'm not getting hard."

"But are you getting wet? Have you touched yourself while replaying it in your head? I bet you have."

"You do realize that you dumped me, like an eternity ago, right? And that under the circumstances, your line of questioning seems rather impertinent."

"If I thought for a second you weren't as hot for me as I am for you I'd let this drop, Harps. But I could tell by the pulse in your throat, the pace of your breath, the moan as you came. You know as well as I do that we've got unfinished business. Why don't we stop wasting time, dispense with the formalities, and get to it already?"

"Harper!" Noah turned to see McDickhead standing there, looking coifed and impeccably stylish.

He nodded at Noah. "Uber driver guy?"

"One and the same," Harper said. "He was just talking

about something. Was it hardball?"

The guy squinted at her trying to get in on the conversation. Conveniently Spencer arrived right in time.

"Ah, Spencer, I want you to meet—" He pointed toward Harper's date.

"Danny," the prick said, extending his hand.

The two exchanged pleasantries while Noah leaned over and whispered into Harper's ear. "Hardball, eh? In fact I was about to tell you how hard I am right now being next to you. And unfortunately you're leaving me with a bad case of blue balls. Because all I want is to bury my hard cock inside of you again."

Harper was midswig when she heard that line and choked as the drink went down.

"Yes, right," she said with a surprisingly straight face. "I'll keep that under advisement for sure."

He extended his hand to shake hers. "Harper. Great to see you again." He dragged his thumb along her palm suggestively before pulling his hand away and nodding toward her date. "Danny. Take good care of the lady."

He smiled a far too toothsome grin. "I have every intention of doing so."

Noah tried hard to suppress the growl that was fighting to escape his throat. He'd have to make sure ole Danny boy didn't take too good care of Harper.

Chapter Fourteen

HARPER and that douchebag had gone off to the restaurant side of the bar, so Noah couldn't even spy on them. He couldn't get his mind off her and what she might do with that loser the whole time he was catching up with Spencer. Which he felt badly about—Spencer was a nice guy.

"This is the chick you dated real seriously way back when?"

"Yeah, we did. But things became complicated."

"Too bad for you. She's a hot piece of ass. I'd do her."

Dagger to the heart. Even nice guys were after Harper. Shit. This was not good. He leaves her to fend for herself in the world, and now the entire male species is getting in line to fuck her?

"Uh, if you'll excuse me for a minute." Noah needed to splash some water on his face. This night was going from bad to super bad. All he wanted was to go home. With Harper. For a command performance. Preferably minus the drama.

He turned down the hallway toward the men's room when he noticed the twerp standing back behind a potted palm tree. He appeared to be on the phone.

"Listen, babe, I swear, I'll be back home tomorrow

afternoon. I promise we can spend the entire day together in bed. Just you and me. Okay? I love you."

Noah blanched. This fucker was two-timing his girl? Who wasn't actually his girl? But needed to be. Or more like he wanted her to be. But she wanted to be Danny's girl. That sounded like a pop song from the eighties, didn't it? Ugh. This had officially become more complicated. He wanted to run out and tell Harper right away, but he knew she'd never believe him. She'd accuse Noah of making shit up. Worse still, she might suggest he was trying to hurt her even more. The thought she'd even accuse him of that made his throat tighten. Not that she had. But she probably would. And she had every reason to, considering how he'd treated her. Oh, man. Poor Harper. How the hell was he going to handle this? It was going to require finesse and nuance. Two qualities he knew he could muster up if need be.

But shit. What if Harper was planning to go home with this guy again? That would be disastrous. He needed to do something to stop her from making a huge mistake.

He circled around the back end of the bar and found the quiet, intimate dining area. Harper was scrolling through Instagram when he came up behind her.

"Listen, Harper—"

"Ack!" She jumped, throwing her hands up and hitting Noah hard in the face. "You scared me!"

Noah reached for his smarting nose and quickly realized it had started to bleed.

"Wow, you've got a good left hook."

Harper turned around and stood up. "Oh, no! I gave you a nosebleed!"

"You punched me, Harper Landry! I bet it felt good!" He reached over and grabbed the napkin from her lap and pressed it to his nose to staunch the flow of blood.

"I didn't punch you! You frightened me. I reacted."

"Nevertheless, I think you need to come back with me to be sure I'm all right."

Her eyes grew wide. "Look, buddy." She pushed her pointer finger into his chest for emphasis. "You killed my chances with Danny last week on our date. I was ready and willing to go home with him for a perfectly lovely night of naked fun and games. Until you came along and screwed that all up."

"At which point you screwed me."

"Which was a mistake made purely in the heat of passion."

"Oh, so you admit you have passion for me."

"It was a generic phrase. What I meant was I was momentarily bitten by the horny bug. No thanks to you."

"Because I stirred up so much passion in you."

"Will you stop with the passion already?" She reached out for the napkin and dabbed at his nose. "I'm sorry about this. Even if I am mad at you—and trust me, I am—I'd never deliberately hurt someone."

"That's good to know. So next time I fall asleep naked next to you, I don't have to worry about any sort of revenge dismemberment then?"

She laughed. "Oh, honey, I had a lot of fantasies of Lorena Bobbitting you, for sure. Good thing I can separate fantasy from reality."

"Can I tell you about the many times I fantasized about you over the past several years?"

She wagged her finger. "Best not to go there. You did this to yourself. There would have been no need to fantasize about me had you stuck around."

Noah saw the two-timing shitmeister approaching

around the corner.

"Listen, I'm serious now. I don't want you going home with him. You have to trust me on this."

"And you don't have any say in who I do or don't sleep with."

"That's true. But I have my reasons. This guy doesn't deserve you, Harps. I can't get into things now, but please. Do not go home with him."

Harper shrugged. "No promises, Noah. Besides," she paused for a minute, "as you're well aware, promises are meant to be broken."

Chapter Fifteen

HARPER felt like maybe that Lorena Bobbitt was onto something with that technique. Because darned if she hadn't been so excited to return to Danny's place, but once again her ex seemed to have cock blocked her (she wondered, can you cock block a woman? Or is that only a guy thing?). Dinner was delightful. Danny regaled her with tales of his triplet nieces who were in kindergarten. And his frazzled sister who was their mother. He talked about how much he traveled for his job. He was headed to Virginia tomorrow for a few days, then up to DC, then back here after that. So if she wanted to strike while the iron was hot, now was the perfect time.

But damn if Noah hadn't been so darned cryptic. It was weird, the way he implored her. As if he knew something she didn't. Though that would be impossible. He didn't even know who Danny was. He was jealous— that had to be it.

She sighed. Ahhh, dammit. It's like Noah was a human candle snuffer, extinguishing her sex drive in the blink of an eye. Except while he quite deftly smothered whatever potential burning embers were there for Danny, he was fanning the veritable conflagration that was flaming up deep in her pelvis the minute she thought about Noah.

His words played on an endless loop in her brain: I was about to tell you how hard I am right now being next to you. And unfortunately you're leaving me with a bad case of blue balls. Because all I want is to bury my hard cock inside of you again.

And all she wanted to do was let him. All. Night. Long.

When Danny returned from paying the check, they left. He offered for Harper to go back with him, but she told him it was late and she was tired. She drove down the darkened beach road to her house, hoping against hope that she'd spy Noah's car waiting out in front of her place. She didn't want to admit she was disappointed he wasn't there.

Good thing she didn't have his phone number. She had enough alcohol in her to loosen her tongue and bolster her bravado, and she'd likely have dialed his number for a booty call of epic proportions that she'd live to regret.

Instead, she'd settle for her pocket rocket and thoughts of Noah pressing himself deep within her wet body. It wasn't nearly as satisfactory but was a far better way to salvage her dignity.

After Noah ran away, Harper had burrowed in for the long haul, spending much of her time crying or preparing to cry or finishing up a cry. Her eyes were so swollen half the time her mother had started fretting that if the tears didn't stop soon, she'd be unable to see. Easy for her to say. Her job search ground to a halt—who would hire someone who looked like a leaf-tailed gecko, all bloodshot and swollen and bulgy-eyed. It was not a "hire me" kind of look.

Besides, it's not as if she could generate the give-a-shit about a career, a future, a life. Her entire foundation had crumbled beneath her feet, and it was gonna take awhile to rebuild whatever she could. She was grateful to her parents for letting her hole up in her bedroom. Her mom worked overtime trying to find something—anything—that Harper would eat. She lost thirty pounds before she knew it, which normally would make any girl slightly thrilled, but in this case, the cost was too high. She'd take the thirty pounds she didn't need to lose right on back if it meant this all hadn't happened.

Allie had taken great care of Harper in those dark days. And she had a group of girlfriends from high school who tried to rally around her, inviting her out for drinks or dinner, the occasional beach bonfire. But soon they drifted away, one by one. You can only take the word "no" so many times before you take it to heart. No one, but maybe Allie, was going to beg her to come out and play. Harper had needed to figure this out herself: how to no longer be Harper and Noah, but instead, plain old Harper.

Months had passed, and she slowly graduated to sitting in the dark watching violent movies on TV. She couldn't muster up the interest in any movie in which a couple even had a one-night stand, let alone an actual relationship. Even in the slasher movies, if there was a couple there, she was yelling at the TV screen, warning the girl about the inevitably untrustworthy guy she was dating, not about the scary masked psychopath with the chainsaw lurking around the corner. Usually she took an odd pleasure in seeing the boyfriend killed. It wasn't a healthy time for Harper Landry.

The only other thing she could abide watching were those awful home-shopping channels. She felt a solidarity knowing that other sad, lonely people were wide awake at 3:00 a.m. debating whether they needed Joan Rivers' pavé Bluebird of Happiness brooch. Because it seemed as if that would be the only happiness she would possess, so maybe she did need to shell out nearly a hundred and fifty bucks for it. Only she didn't have a hundred and fifty bucks. Her bank account was as bare bones as Harper's body was.

One day, after seeing Joan Rivers' QVC jewelry show for about the fortieth time, she had a revelation. She didn't need the Joan Rivers enamel Rose Garden Statement necklace. She wasn't even clear on what a statement necklace was and whether she had a statement to make. She didn't want Joan's simulated Opal and Crystal Beetle brooch. She hated beetles—why would she want to wear it as a fashion statement? And truthfully, she was pavé'd out. But she was bored. And inspired.

After all, Joan Rivers didn't come into this world a jewelry maven, yet here she was making a fortune with it. Harper had always had a crafty side: for instance, she knitted a mean sweater—sadly, she'd made Noah several over the years. And she wanted them back, dammit. She was sorely tempted to march over to his house and ask his mother to pony them up. But going to the Gunderson home would only sadden her, so instead, she hoped that his closet would become infested with moths so they'd eat the sweaters and be happy.

Harper had even dabbled in making jewelry at summer camp. She made so many of those embroidery thread bracelets she'd started selling them and did a brisk business during lunch break in middle school. Her handiwork was showcased on wrists throughout the population of Verity Beach Junior High School, home of the Fighting Seahorses. Seriously, that was their mascot. Well, if she could successfully manipulate all of those tiny threads into complicated patterns as a tween, surely now as a full-grown adult she could figure out how to make real jewelry that women her age would want. No pavé for her; rather she was going to make beachy, natural-looking jewelry that she'd want to wear.

At first she made simpler beaded things: drop earrings, bracelets, necklaces. But as her interest grew, she started taking classes and learned how to make her own silver jewelry. Her parents were just happy she had started washing her hair on a regular basis, and her father was downright elated when she started trying to sell her creations, being that they were taking up most of the space in the family dining room.

She opened an Etsy store and started marketing her products with ads on Facebook, and soon, her designs took off. She was receiving so many orders she had to find someone to help her manage the sales and shipping. And her parents gently encouraged her to find somewhere other than their home to create her masterpieces.

Harper decided it made sense to open a storefront. This was the beach, after all. Tourist mecca for three-quarters of the year. People always seemed to love to buy jewelry when on vacation at the beach. A perfect marriage of need and fulfillment. And probably the only marriage she'd ever be committed to at this point. But she was okay with that. At least she'd finally found a purpose. She sure wasn't in the mood to find a man anytime soon—if ever— but she was excited to discover her passion, and her shop,

Designs by Harper had taken off so well that she was able to move out of her parents' place and into her own at last. And she was fine settling for unlucky in love, kick-ass in business. She didn't need Noah Gunderson to lead a fulfilling life.

Chapter Sixteen

Noah sat relishing his morning coffee on the terrace overlooking the ocean, where a brilliant melon-hued ball of fire was cresting over the horizon. At this time of day, he was always at his best. He'd already been out surfing and was now strategizing his schedule in anticipation of the wedding the inn was hosting this evening.

These events always made him a little nervous, probably more so as they'd been negotiated by his mother long before he'd taken over the place. Bit by bit, her bookings had mostly come and gone, and he was already doing a steady business of booking events into the following year. But he wanted to do right by his mother and keep her legacy alive, so he was conscientious about trying to do things her way. Ultimately he wanted to transition into managing the place in the way he was most comfortable, but for now, he followed her plan of operation line by line, and in a way, her guidance was a reassuring hug from afar.

He hadn't expected to enjoy being an innkeeper. It seemed so odd for a man of his young age to do so. Seemed like the type of job a retiree might take on. But after running the place for this long, he was grateful he didn't wait until he was older. This was hard work: there were always repairs that needed to be done in the historic building. It seemed Mother Nature wanted to encroach on his little patch of land, with leaks here and there a regular occurrence. Soon he'd have to figure out how to replace the roof, but in the meantime, he'd been able to bandage together repairs enough to stave off that large expense.

Perhaps his taking over his mother's money pit was a blessing in disguise. In all the traveling he'd done, perhaps the thing he loved the most was hospitality of strangers who made him feel at home even when he was oceans away from his real home. A mother's touch, a comfortable bed, a home-cooked breakfast, a warm shower: all of these things may have seemed insignificant, but ultimately when you're far from home, they mattered so much. And maybe somehow this was his mother's gift to him, this legacy she passed on so he could extend that same sense of warmth and welcoming that was so important to him, to other travelers who might need a welcoming place to settle into or at least a psychological hug.

It sure beats practicing law, he thought with a laugh.

Sometimes he thought about the law degree he never completed. He wondered if he was a quitter, and that concerned him. Was he? He up and quit Harper with nary a glance backward. Ditto with law school. Though for two very different reasons. And if he honestly examined it, he'd admit he'd glanced back plenty. At Harper. Not at the relationship itself. That bit was what made him so damned scared. Harper? He would have been happy keeping things the way they'd been. She was the person who made him happiest in the world. But happy didn't mean forever, did it?

The idea that he could get stuck like Matt, his whole future having to be rolled up like a dirty rug, all of those plans, those fun things forfeited because of a slip-up, was like a cold bucket of ice water dropped on his head. Ugh. That had been the thing he selfishly focused on. Because when he was twenty-one, the idea of being tied down like Gulliver by the Lilliputians was downright terrifying. Now? It no longer instilled the fear of God in him. In fact, after having spent time with that little bugger Tyler, he kind of liked the idea. Sure kids were a lot of work, but they were also rewarding. It's too bad the timing was so backward on this revelatory notion. Now, the idea of having a little Tyler-type Lilliputian with Harper almost put butterflies in his stomach. In a good way.

He'd hoped that his running away—and let's face it, it was absolutely running away sans the bandana full of belongings tied to the end of a hobo stick and balanced on his shoulder—would lead to some soul-searching. And indeed it did. In India, he meditated beneath the scorching hot sun until his skin could take it no more. In Tibet, he contributed to the building and—necessary—destruction of beautiful sand mandalas. It pained him to deconstruct what took many monks and helpers like him weeks to craft, but that was the point of it all: to emphasize the ephemeral nature of life. He channeled energy at Machu Picchu. He stood at sunrise fixing his gaze on the magnificent statues at Easter Island, marveling at the unexplainable. He communed with aboriginal tribesmen at Uluru in Australia.

Now in truth, some of this wasn't quite as glamorous as it sounded. In Tibet, he also spent a week puking his guts up with a mysterious ailment, only to be made well with the help of a Tibetan healer. He picked up nasty bedbugs at the hostel he stayed at before he made the week-long hike up the Andes Mountains to Machu Picchu. And he was bitten by hundreds of ants as he slept beneath the stars near Uluru.

But it was all worth it. Noah left a boy but returned a man—one who had seen the world and experienced mental and physical hardship, growing greatly in the process. He'd tested and learned his limits, learned to respect his fear and admire his bravery.

And now here he was in a more pedestrian world, back home almost as if he'd never left. Running an inn. Preparing for a lovely union of yet another happy couple. He always wondered a little bit about people who went into marriage with blinders on, only able to see how joyful they were at that snapshot in time, naïve to think they'd get through a lifetime together untainted. There was a time that probably would have stopped him from ever moving forward in a relationship—even one as serious as what he and Harper shared. He'd always assumed that his father and mother were equally smitten with one another when they were young, so that didn't help instill confidence in the institution. It wasn't until his mother was sick and dying that she confessed the truth about his parentage: they hadn't been young and in love. His mother and father had had a one-night stand that took a bad turn when she got pregnant. His father was never on board with the whole thing but gave it a go for a while. He'd been young and irresponsible and didn't actually even like Noah's mother, let alone love her. It wasn't enough to keep him around.

Noah sometimes felt bad that his father didn't want him and Matthew, but he could also understand it, intellectually. Just as he had freaked out on behalf of his very brother. One thing he knew: parenthood was not for the faint of heart.

But now each time he oversaw another wedding at the inn, he smiled and sent his warm wishes into the universe that the couple would weather their particular storms and grow stronger. He'd seen it with his own eyes with Matt and Katie, so he knew that a deep foundation of love could help two people get through tough circumstances.

He wished he could get Harper to understand the Noah he was now, to realize that he was an improved version of the one she fell in love with when they were children. Maybe someday she'd come around.

Chapter Seventeen

HARPER hit a shot of hot air from her blow dryer onto her eyelash curler, then squeezed the thing over her eyelashes. She only did this on important occasions—half the time when she used that damned contraption she ended up with an eye injury. Nothing more attractive than a big red mark from a pinched eyelid. But it did result in a much nicer-looking set of eyelashes, and it beat attempting those fake ones again, which was a disaster last time. Not that it would matter where she was going, but she wanted to give it her best. She was going to be the plus-one for her assistant, Georgia Childress, at the wedding of Georgia's cousin Marcy.

"Dude. I need reinforcements," had said. "My cousin's fine enough, but her mother is a primo A-number-one beyotch. She'll be so busy gloating about her daughter and her perfect marriage and dreamboat husband and bragging that Marcy was able to find someone but oh, *poor Georgia, maybe you'll find someone someday.*" She put that last bit in air quotes. "I can't stand being in the same room with her, and today of all days, I need someone to grab me by the shoulders and pull me away from her in case I feel the need to deck her."

Harper adored Georgia—she was tall and well filled

out. Not fat but certainly no petite shrinking flower of a woman. She brooked no bullshit from anyone and she sort of filled her body well with her sassy personality. She could care less that she wasn't married, but she cared a whole lot that her aunt wanted to flaunt it. Harper wasn't usually much on weddings for obvious reasons. But to go as a bodyguard? Sounded perfect.

She pulled on the form-fitting navy satin bias-cut slip dress that fell right above the knees and made her legs look a mile long, slicked on a couple of layers of mascara, pulled her hair back in a ponytail, slid into a pair of silver strap-heeled sandals, and checked herself in the mirror.

"Not bad," she said, nodding at what she saw. "Not bad at all."

Georgia—Georgie for short—insisted on driving and picked her up about fifteen minutes before the six o'clock wedding was scheduled to begin. "Hoping if we get there late enough we'll get the seats farthest as possible from my aunt," she said as Harper pulled on her seatbelt.

Harper would be happy to miss the ceremony altogether—each wedding she attended felt a little bit like salt in an old wound. Sure, she'd made it past the whole Noah thing in a general sense, but still, it was always hard to not reflect on what could have been. And now it was even harder because of the lust-filled way she'd so recently been reminded. So much so that she'd been running down the batteries on her vibrator, it had become such a necessary appliance in her life over the past few weeks. It seemed like every night when she tried to fall asleep, all she could think of was what had transpired between the two of them. And what red-blooded girl wouldn't then feel the need to act upon that? It wasn't as if she could call him up and demand round two.

They parked about a block from the inn where the wedding was being held.

As the venue came into view, Harper admired it. "Cute old home," she said, eyeing the sprawling, pale lavender Victorian-style house with the inviting wraparound front porch. "I didn't even know this place existed. And look"— she pointed to the roof—"a widow's walk. They're so romantic. The whole place screams charming."

"Of course it does," her friend said. "Leave it to my Aunt Jeannie to find the perfect, most romantic venue that no one else even knows about. God forbid her precious spawn marry at a venue others have used."

Harper laughed. "Man, you love that woman, don't you?"

"It's only that she's always put me and Marcy in a competition and I hated it. Left to our own devices, we could have been good friends. But with her mother adding that layer of 'my daughter's better than you,' it was pretty much a doomed friendship from the get-go."

Harper reached for her hand and pulled her toward the steps. "Well, you look absolutely ravishing." And she did: her blond hair was pulled into a French braid that highlighted her soft, blue eyes. She wore a silver silk dress with a flared sheer floral silver organza overlay. The high-waisted dress was scooped at the neck and landed midcalf. She had on the most amazing glittery silver pumps. Harper pointed at her feet. "Oh, man. Those shoes. I have serious shoe envy, you know."

Georgie stuck out her foot and wiggled it. "I borrowed them from my mom's best friend, Margie. Margie said she knew my mom would've bought me something equally dazzling if she were around to do so."

"Aww, that's so sweet. I love that you have her in your

life."

She nodded. "Tell me about it. You can't put a price tag on moral support."

Which was true. Harper still had her parents, though she tried not to lean on them. She'd done enough leaning on them for that first year after being dumped, so when she finally rose from the ashes, she savored her independence. She got along with them just fine, but she tried to give them space. Plus they traveled so much they were rarely in town anymore. All good, though. Harper had a wonderful network of friends and had carved out a lovely life for herself.

They entered the inn, which was spacious yet cozy, with two overstuffed floral-patterned sofas facing an inviting fire crackling in a large fireplace. An older woman ushered them through a second room with tables set up for the reception, out toward an expansive tented deck space that overlooked the ocean. Hundreds of lit candles twinkled both outside and inside the clear-sided tent.

Harper was partial to ocean-front views. The sand and the surf spoke to her, and ever since she was a little girl, it was a place she associated with joy. She and Noah had spent lots of time on the beach, both by day and night. It was the perfect place for a little late-night delight when there weren't many quiet places to go parking in. They must've known every private beach cove for a good twenty-mile stretch of beach.

When they reached the door to exit onto the deck, someone opened the door for them.

"Welcome, ladies," a man said. But not any man. *That* man. The man she so didn't want to hear, even though she really did. Harper looked up to see Noah in a smart charcoal business suit with a crisp white button-down and a magenta-and-gray diagonally striped tie. She wondered for a second if he was the first course or the second course for dinner tonight. Because he looked good enough to eat, though she couldn't let him know that's what she was thinking.

She cocked her eyebrow at him. "Is this your day job or something?"

He shrugged. "You could say that."

"Okay, then. So you're a wedding usher by day, Uber driver by night. Interesting." She nodded her head.

"Funny that we hadn't gotten around to discussing our chosen career paths yet. I guess we've been too busy with more pressing matters." He winked at her, and she was torn between wanting to punch him or kiss him. Or both. She was beginning to see there was a fine line between love and hate. Except this wasn't love. That was then. This was pure, unadulterated lust. And she was good with that. She was perfectly happy to employ him as her itch scratcher. She deserved that, at the very least. Plus it could save her a ton on batteries.

Georgie looked at Harper, then at Noah. "So you two know each other?"

Harper had been busy staring at Noah in a suit, which was almost as big a turn-on as Noah without his pants on. She'd yet to encounter the full Monty since he'd been home, at least, but the suit was a completely perfect stand-in for a thoroughly naked Noah. She nodded slowly then turned to Georgie. "Sorry. Didn't mean to be rude. Georgie, meet Noah."

Georgie knit her brows. "Noah as in *that* Noah?"

Harper so wished she hadn't said that. It meant Harper had told Georgie all about him, and she wanted Noah to think she was long ago over him.

"This is the Noah I might have mentioned before."

Georgie shook his hand as if she'd touched something hot. "Damn, girl, you failed to tell me that he looked like this. No wonder you were pissed at him leaving."

The corner of Noah's mouth curled up into a grin. He reached his hand out. "Georgie—delighted to meet you. How do you two beautiful women know each other?"

Beautiful women. What a suck-up.

"I'm Harper's right-hand woman in the shop."

"Oh? What shop is that?"

Georgie threw a side glance at her friend. "He doesn't even know about the shop?"

Harper frowned. "Um, no?"

"I'd love to hear more about this mystery shop."

Harper shook her head. "Stop mocking me. There's nothing mysterious about it. I simply didn't want to share my private business with you. I reserve that for people I trust."

Georgie licked the tip of her finger and tapped the air, making a sizzling sound. "The score: Harper, one. Noah, zero."

The background music started to get louder, indicating the wedding was about to begin. Noah showed them to their seats—lucky for Georgie they were in the back row. Unlucky for Harper, she was on the end, and the bride no sooner walked down the short aisle than Noah came and hovered right next to her like he was her bodyguard. If she dared turn to her left, her eyes would be about level with his crotch.

At first she nonchalantly held her program up, attempting to obscure her line of vision. But then her curiosity got the better of her and when she thought he wasn't looking, she lowered the paper and glanced out of the corner of her eyes; it was impossible not to notice how very big he looked in his sexy hipster suit pants. Heat rushed to her face and she knew her cheeks had turned a charming shade of tomato-red. Made worse because Noah then angled his body slightly toward her head, giving her a bird's-eye view of his thickening Johnson. She looked up at exactly the wrong time, as he was obviously watching her reaction. He grinned.

So much for being Georgia's bodyguard. She was going to need her own to withstand the wiles of the omnipresent Noah Gunderson.

Chapter Eighteen

NOAH couldn't believe his good fortune to have Harper as a guest at this wedding. Now he needed to figure out a way to worm his way into her conversations all night. The cheating doofus wasn't with her, and that was a good sign that. Noah wondered where he was and why he wasn't her plus-one. But why worry about it? Rather, he planned to take advantage of it.

He approached Harper and her friend as they mingled inside the heated tent following the ceremony. "Can I get you ladies a cocktail?"

Harper rolled her eyes at Georgie, but her friend was having none of it. "I'd love a Tito's on the rocks with a splash of sparkling water and a lime."

He looked at his ex who shrugged. "I don't know. Surprise me."

Oh, he was planning to surprise her, all right.

He went to the bartender and ordered up two drinks, returning with them a few minutes later.

"Your vodka," he said, handing Georgie her cocktail.

"And for you, something I thought would be a fun reminder of one of our favorite pastimes." He held up a drink the color of the morning sunrise he'd witnessed earlier in the day.

"I don't get it," Harper said.

He leaned over and whispered into her ear. "Sex on the beach." He winked at her and walked away, leaving Harper momentarily speechless.

A few minutes later, Noah ran into his friend.

"Spencer," he said, patting him on the back. "I didn't know you'd be at this wedding. You sure clean up well."

Usually the two of them saw each other in wetsuits. When not on a surfboard, Spencer was often found on a bicycle, as he was a courier by day and far preferred biking to his delivery destinations than driving a car. Tonight he had his longish sandy-blond hair pulled back in a sort of ponytail-bun. *A bunny tail!* She laughed to herself.

"Every now and then I take one for the team. But you know me, I'd much rather be dripping wet right now."

"Funny you should say that." He pointed toward Harper. "I'd much prefer that she was dripping wet as well." The two of them laughed.

"I don't blame you there."

"Yeah, well, maybe you can help me then."

Spencer lifted a brow. "Dude, really? Me and her? Like I'd be the fluffer only for the woman?"

Noah pinched the bridge of his nose with his thumb and forefinger. "You might want to consider it more like wingman, with benefits. I'm going to introduce you to Harper's friend who you are going to take a liking to, which will give me a chance to get Harper alone. Got it?"

He shrugged. "Sure, I can do that. Though what's in it for me?"

Noah nodded toward Georgie, whose back was to them. "Maybe her friend?"

Spencer stuck out his lower lip, thinking. "Hey, I'd do her."

"And you have my complete endorsement. The longer you keep her away, the better for me."

By this point at an event, his staff had things well under control. He only needed to figure out the prime opportunity to waylay Harper and employ his charms on her. Surely he'd have the chance.

He motioned with his finger for Spencer to follow him.

"Look who I found all alone and needing company," Noah said, his hand on Spencer's shoulder. "Harper, I think you might recall meeting Spencer at the bar, right?"

Harper reached out to shake his hand. "Great to see you again. And this is my date for this evening, Georgie Childress."

Spencer reached for Georgie's hand and pulled it toward his mouth. "Enchanté," he said, as he kissed the top of her hand.

"Uhhh, yeah," Georgie said squinting her eyes. "You seriously don't remember me?"

He lifted a brow, then winced as he started to snap his fingers. "Oh, man. You. Surfboard-killer chick."

.Harper looked from her friend to Spencer. "Should I ask?"

Georgia shook her head. "Trust me, it's so not worth knowing."

Harper shrugged. "Okey dokey, then." She mouthed to her friend *you'd better fill me on on that later.*

The wedding director began to announce the bridal party, who had gone down to the beach to take photographs, which was weird because it was November and the sun had already set, but whatever.

"I'll leave you three to find your seats while I see to it that everyone gets their meal in a timely way." Noah ushered the three of them toward a table, ensuring that Spencer would sit next to his prey for the evening.

With any luck, his plan would be as easy as feeding candy to a baby.

Noah felt a load of relief once the tables had all been bussed. Now all that was left was dancing and mingling and wedding cake, so he could buck that to his helpers to make sure it all went smoothly.

From the far end of the room, he'd been keeping an eye on Harper. She seemed like she was having a good time, smiling and laughing. He was glad she hadn't latched on to any young, available male guests.

He wondered if weddings were stressful for her. If so, he felt like a real heel for it. But that was water under the bridge. It was time for him to build a new bridge or some such metaphor. At last he saw Harper get up and head toward the steps, presumably in search of the ladies' room. He took his cue and slipped up the back steps where he'd be able to intercept her.

He watched from the shadows as she closed the door to the bathroom, and then he waited. This was going to be fun.

Chapter Nineteen

HARPER was a bit wedding'd out. It was a lovely event, even though she didn't know the bride. And she certainly didn't want to know the mother of the bride. At least spending time with Georgie had been fun, though weirdly she and the surfer dude seemed to have some strange history she was going to need to find out about. She kept getting the sense Georgie wanted to give the guy the slip. Maybe it was the occasional wince she threw her way when it seemed Spencer wasn't looking. Even so, Harper had felt like a third wheel, a sensation she didn't adore. It was one thing to be on your own—she was good with that. But it became uncomfortable when you were with others who were paired off—even if those two weren't necessarily paired off. It still made her feel like an extra appendage, one of those additional fingers people sometimes have: needless, yet there and sort of in the way.

Harper had only excused herself to take a moment to regroup. Maybe the two of them would want to dance or at least not have her be a necessary part of the conversation while they were getting to know each other. She was happy for her friend—Georgie deserved to have a fun time with a guy. Presuming she wanted to have fun with him. But she didn't want to be a fly on the wall. She washed her hands and was walking down the hall, resolved to find a ride home when she heard that voice.

"I've discovered I have a bit of a thing for sexy sandals," Noah said as he approached her. He reached his hands to her shoulders, then leaned over and whispered in her ear. "Especially when they're attached to a gorgeous woman with the most beautiful tits." He took a deep breath and let it out. "Not that I'm getting enough of a look at those breasts, I'm so stuck on the sandals." His hands slid down to cup her breasts as he steered her backward toward a nearby linen storage room.

Once inside, he slid his thumbs under the edge of her bodice to find her nipples already hard. He groaned and settled his mouth over hers as his tongue pressed past her lips in search of her tongue. The pace of her breathing increased, and she couldn't suppress a moan when he pinched her nipples hard.

"You like it when I do that?" He dragged his lips down her chin, along her throat while he slipped the slinky straps of her dress over her shoulders.

"You know I do."

"What else do you like?" His mouth trailed down along her collarbone, and he painted his tongue toward a waiting nipple, pinching the areola as his lips latched on and he suckled.

"That."

"What?" he said on a murmur.

"I love when you suck on me."

"Where?" One hand reached behind her, quickly tugging the zipper of the dress down.

Her breathing was at a fevered pitch. "I love it when you suck on my nipples."

He bit down hard on one nipple and Harper shouted

out. He quickly covered her mouth with his hand. "Shhh. I can keep going as long as we don't get caught out. I don't want the grandmother of the bride to walk in on us when I'm thrusting my cock inside of you."

Harper groaned at the mere notion of that. She wanted it there so badly.

He pulled her dress down, and it pooled at her feet. Noah looked at the floor.

"The only sight better than those sandals is your dress settled down around them." His voice was gravelly. "You want to know why?"

"Tell me why."

"Because that means that I get to stare at those fucking tits and suck on them as much as I want, and I know you want it as badly as I do."

He pulled back for a moment and cast a long, slow gaze over her mostly naked body. He let out a quiet whistle. "Damn, Harper," he said. "You're even more beautiful than I remember. We need to do one more thing."

He reached down and tugged with one finger on the skimpy black lace panties that barely covered her, pulling them down to her ankles and helping her step out of them.

"Such a pretty sight, I might come in my pants." He slid his fingers along her pussy, stroking the neatly trimmed thatch of hair that barely covered her. "I can see your swollen clit peeking out from your lips." He stroked along her lips, circling her clit again and again. "And you're so wet."

Harper spread her legs. She couldn't believe ten minutes ago she was ready to go home and now she was naked in a large storage closet with Noah running color commentary on her aroused and very naked body.

He reached for her wrists and hoisted them up over

her head as his fingers explored her wet pussy, sliding toward her center. He hooked a finger inside her while he used his palm to continue to stimulate her clit. Harper gasped.

"How do you know I love that?" she choked the words out, pressing herself toward his hand, forcing his finger deeper inside of her to that perfect spot.

Noah's eyes were fixed on what his hands were doing, and Harper couldn't help but watch as well, mesmerized. To think that those fingers could make her feel such intense pleasure. She writhed as the sensations bombarded her, all the while wanting desperately to strip his clothes off and feel him pressed up against her naked flesh.

"I remember everything your body wants, baby. And I plan to give it to you."

"Clothes," she said between gasps. "Off. Now."

"Uh-uh." Noah held tight to her wrists and leaned forward to lick her nipple. He increased the pace of his finger thrusting into her, pressing the heel of his hand to her clit, spreading her juices, occasionally rubbing the swollen nub with his thumb. "First I need to feel you come all over my hand." He added a second finger and Harper thrust desperately against him. When he fastened his mouth around a nipple and bit down as he pressed his fingers to her G-spot, a thousand points of light burst behind Harper's eyelids as wave upon wave of spasms racked her pelvis. She let out a gasp, but Noah closed his mouth over hers to stifle the sound as his hand slowed over her sensitive lips. Finally he released her wrists.

Harper felt like she'd run a marathon. But she was ready for an ultramarathon, at least of the sexual kind, and immediately grabbed his tie, unknotting it in record time, then his suitcoat, unfastening his shirt, and ultimately his pants. She stopped to smooth the precum that had gathered at the head of his cock as she slid the waistband of his boxer briefs over his hard length. She'd always loved the velvety smoothness of Noah's cock, the firm thickness, the length. He was built just right for her, and she couldn't believe she was here, once again holding it in her greedy little hands.

She squatted down, still in her strappy heels, and looked up at Noah, reaching her tongue out to lick the moisture from the head. His sharp intake of breath was all she needed to know that this was what he craved. She circled the crown with her tongue before wrapping her lips around the head and slowly sliding them down his penis, taking the length of him into her mouth as he pressed toward her.

She sucked him hard and took him as deep as she could, then alternated stroking her tongue along the length of him as he guided her head with desperate hands. When she covered her teeth with her lips and pressed along the crown, he cried out, "Oh, fuck, Harper. I want you, now."

He reached his hands under her armpits and pulled her up, and they coiled in an embrace as Harper lifted a leg around his hip, trying to encourage his hard length into her wetness.

"I have a better idea." He turned her around and bent her at the waist, her naked ass pointed toward him. "Those shoes. Those fuck-me shoes. God, Harper, if you only knew what those did to me." With one stroke he was inside of her, buried deep, where he held himself, allowing her body to adjust to his size. "We fit together like we were made to for each other, sweetie."

She shuddered at the intensity of his large, magnificent cock inside her, right where it always belonged. "Harder,

Noah."

He obliged, first leaning forward, his chest to her back, and wrapping his arms around her body so he could play with her nipples the way she loved it. She trembled, so close to breaking again, relishing the feel of his body sliding inside of her, the soft hairs of his chest stroking her back. She could do this forever, except that it felt like a fuse had been lit and was quickly snaking through her body, and the blast was imminent. Noah reached down and slid his fingers along her slick center, reaching to the spot where his cock was sliding in and out of her body, then swirling around her clit. It was all Harper could take.

"I'm coming, baby, now," she said. "Come with me." Fireworks erupted inside of her, and her pussy clamped down hard on his cock, pulling him in. She could feel his body spasming as she milked the seed from his pulsating cock, filling her to overflowing.

For a minute they were silent but for their labored breathing. Then Harper started to laugh, and Noah joined in.

"You do know you have an inn full of wedding guests downstairs, while you've been fucking my brains out up here?"

Her legs had given out, and as he slipped from her body, she turned and lay herself down on the carpeted floor.

Noah settled himself down next to her, breathing heavily. "God, I didn't think my legs had enough strength to remain standing for another second." He leaned forward and stroked her face. "Besides, it's much nicer down here." He pulled her mouth toward his and their tongues met and tangled, softly, gently, in a kiss so tender Harper thought she could cry. This was what she missed the most. All the other stuff, sure, she missed it. But intimate moments like this, with the man she'd long ago given her heart to. It was a real shame she could never give that heart away again.

Chapter Twenty

NOAH'S eyes searched Harper's hoping to find some intent behind what transpired. Had they just had astonishingly great sex? Or was it something more than that? Was there still love on her side? He knew there was for him. Now more than ever. And it wasn't that boyish love from before but rather a tender, deeper, more mature love that he wasn't capable of when he was younger.

His fingers traced along her body as they lay on their sides, facing each other.

"Don't you think you'd better get back downstairs in case things have exploded in your absence?"

He grinned. "Hate to tell you, but things already exploded in my presence. And yours." His face fell as did hers.

"Crap," she said.

"Double crap," he said.

"No condom," they said in unison.

"Should I be worried?" she asked.

"Look, Harper, if you were to get pregnant, you know I'd be there for you."

She shook her head. This reminded her of what she'd conveniently forgotten until now: Noah's little boy. Noah of all people must know about failed protection methods.

"I meant am I going to catch anything from you?"

Noah started to laugh, quietly. "Harper, I haven't slept with a woman in longer than I can remember."

"That's odd. Why not?"

He fixed an earnest gaze on hers. "Because I realized I wanted to be with you."

She laughed. "Oh, that's rich."

He frowned. "What?"

"Kind of too little, too late, don't you think? All these years later."

"It's never too late, Harps. You feel it, I know you do. I hear it in the tiny whimper you make when I suck on your nipple. I hear it in the gasp of pleasure you release on that first amazing press of my cock inside of you. I see it when you stroke your tongue along my cock while you lock eyes with me. I know you feel it, Harper."

She frowned, thinking about that little boy he was hiding from her. Where was the mother? Did he have a relationship with her as well? "Sorry, Noah. You're wrong about that. It's exactly as I told you: I've been in this long, dry spell. And you're simply watering my garden, remember?"

He shrugged. "Have it your way. But remember, with enough water, you might be surprised at what blooms."

They got dressed, dreadfully rumpled now, and returned to the wedding reception, the trickling of warm semen down her leg a reminder of what happened, almost chastising her for lying as she had. She wasn't merely using Noah for the sex, but she was too damned afraid to ever get past the superficial with him and truly share herself, her body, her heart, her emotions.

Wouldn't you know, Georgie was nowhere to be found. Same went for Spencer. Which meant Harper's chariot had turned into a pumpkin. Hell, she could've saved herself a lot of, well, whatever happened between them a few minutes ago, if she knew she was going to be ditched. She could've found another ride and been in bed by now.

But then again, deep down, she wished she could be in bed by now with the man who was nearby standing with an older woman ruminating about something on a clipboard the woman was holding. Harper knew if she actually had him in bed for the night, she would lose her tight control over things, including her emotions. And that would be entirely unacceptable.

Harper leaned back against the wall, trying to do a discreet—so as not to look desperate— search for Georgie before she bailed herself. An older woman in a floral dress and sensible shoes with short gray hair and warm brown eyes sidled up beside her. "Aren't you our Noah's friend?"

Harper looked at her with suspicion. Who was she and why would she call her "our" Noah's friend. And who the hell was the "us" she must've been referring to? Harper decided to remain polite, hoping the woman would soon go away. She extended her hand. "Hi. I'm Harper Landry. I guess long ago and far away I was your Noah's friend. Or more than friend. Whatever you'd call it."

The woman smiled. "I've heard so much about you, dear." She shook her head as if forgetting something. "I'm Betty Lipscomb. Martha"—she pointed to the tall woman with the long gray plait and black dress with whom Noah was talking to—"and I stayed on to help Noah transition the inn."

"Transition the place? I thought he was just working here."

She waved her hands. "Oh, heavens no. Noah is the owner."

Harper squinted, confused. "Where would he get the money to buy an inn? And why would he want to tie himself down like that? I'm sure it's no secret to you that he's not one to stick around."

Betty sighed. "I know that was your experience." She placed a hand on her shoulder. "It must have been heartbreaking."

Harper wasn't exactly prepared to spill her guts to this gal. But she seemed so warm and kind and thoughtful. "It was awful. Horrible. Shifted the earth beneath my feet. Took me years to collect myself and even think about opening up to people again. Killed my sense of trust."

Betty pulled her into a hug, which was weird but lovely all at once. "I'm sorry," she said. "Boys sometimes do the dumbest things."

Ugh, if she wasn't careful, she might start crying. Something about confessionals with strangers.

"You never explained how it is he owns this place."

"Millie—Noah's mother—bought the place shortly after he went away. What with Noah gone, and then Matt and Katie moved in with her folks—"

"Wait. Matt and Katie moved in with her family? Why?"

"Well, because of the baby. It made sense. Katie had more family who could help out with Tyler once he was born."

Harper shook her head. "Who's Tyler?"

"Matt and Katie's boy."

"I'm sorry but how did I miss out on that news?"

Betty shrugged. "Don't ask me. Maybe you didn't want to hear any of it?"

It was true. She'd shunned Millie. She hadn't appreciated how lonely Millie must've been as well, with her firstborn so suddenly long gone.

"Millie had a big heart but she hadn't a clue about keeping a place like this in the black. I think she hoped this would be her little nest egg, and eventually she could retire here, maybe her grandchildren would come and play."

"What happened?"

"She started losing weight, got sick suddenly, and declined rapidly. The cancer had taken over her body. The minute he knew something was wrong, Noah left law school and raced home to help out with his mama."

"Wait. You're telling me Noah was in law school?"

She nodded. "But I think he was looking for an excuse to leave."

Harper frowned. "Yep. Sounds like him."

Betty shook her head. "I didn't mean that in a negative way. I only meant he found out it wasn't for him."

Same way he'd found out Harper wasn't, probably.

"How long was he in law school for?"

"He was in his second year when he came home. Nursed Millie through that terrible time. And as she lay dying, he promised her he'd fix this place. Make it so that it was financially viable. He's been running the inn ever since."

"I'm so sorry about Millie," Harper said, wiping a tear from her eye. "She was always so sweet. I had a soft spot in my heart for her. But after Noah left, I simply couldn't—"

Betty placed a hand on her shoulder again. "Of course not. I'm sure Millie didn't take it personally. She understood these things."

Betty pointed at the floral arrangements on the table. "Noah's tried to honor his mother's wishes right down to the décor for each wedding. She had these things planned out long ago, before she got sick. Not great with budgeting but she had an eye for details. So Noah has followed her instructions to the T, making sure the weddings he's creating here are exactly what Millie dreamed of."

Wow. She had made him out to be an ogre in her mind after all this time. She'd wanted to see him hurt like he'd hurt her. The only way she could hurt him was with her words, so she had been fine saying things that would ensure he knew she didn't care about him. But dammit, how could she not? The man this woman Betty was talking about was a kind, thoughtful, deliberative man. Not a boy who would flee from responsibility. Even if she still didn't know why he did what he did. This was a lot to absorb. She wasn't quite sure how to process it.

Locking arms with Harper, Betty led her to where Noah was standing.

"Martha—what say you and I take care of closing everything up tonight? I think this young lady needs a ride and I know exactly the man to help her out." She gently pushed Harper toward Noah and ushered them both toward the front door.

Harper couldn't yell at a sweet old gal like that, so she obliged her, all the while wondering exactly what she was getting herself into. It seemed a far cry from a little itch scratching, that was for sure.

Chapter Twenty-One

"SO I guess I have no choice in the matter about your driving me home?"

"Not unless you want to insult my mom's two best friends."

"Far be it from me to buzzkill those sweet women."

"Yep. That's been my experience as well. If the world had more people like those two, there would be no wars. Who could ever confront them? They're a force of nature."

Harper laughed, but then rested her hand on his.

"Betty told me about your mother." She looked at him, her damp eyes reflecting the lights of an oncoming car. Those eyes he'd thought about so many times over the years. "Must have been awful."

"More than you can imagine."

"I wish I had known about her passing. I would have come to the funeral." She sighed. "I mean, I'd made myself scarce with your mother. I had to. But had I known—"

"How could you have? Had I known, I'd have done things differently too."

"I hadn't appreciated that when you left me, you left her too. Maybe it was even harder on her."

"Oh, I don't know. I think I caused enough pain to go around."

Harper laughed softly. "More than you can imagine." She parroted his words deliberately. Taking a deep breath, she prepared herself for the question she never thought she'd get a chance to ask. "Why'd you leave?"

They pulled up to her place and he put the car in park. He turned to look at her, scrubbing his hands over his face. "Do you mind if I come in to continue this conversation?"

She nodded, opening her door and getting out. This time she unlocked the front door with less drama than last time, reaching out her hand and offering it to his as she walked inside.

She then motioned for him to have a seat on the sofa.

"I'm going to ask you something, and you can feel free to say no, Harps." He pursed his lips, afraid she'd say no.

"Go right ahead." She nodded.

"If we're going to have this talk, can we do it in bed? Naked?" He held up his hands as if in defeat. "Not because I want to make love to you—even though of course I do—but because I want this to be a bare-bones, intimate conversation, nothing held back. I want to be able to hold you as tightly to me as I can, to let you know exactly where I'm coming from and why I did what I did. If after all that, you want to kick me out, I'll leave, no questions asked."

Harper stared at him, squinting as if she wondered if this was some sort of trick. He could hardly blame her.

He removed his coat and helped her with hers, then reached out to clasp her hand in his. He nodded. "Lead the way."

They walked down a short hallway into a large bedroom decorated in shades of white. The bed contained more pillows than a bed ought to hold, but he had to admit it looked inviting. Not nearly as alluring as it would with a naked Harper in it, though.

"So, uh, how do we go about this? Minus the seduction, I don't quite know the protocol for getting naked with your ex-boyfriend who abruptly ditched you but then with whom you've decided to have tawdry booty call sex, except this time the plan is for skin on skin, but evidently no skin in skin? Do I have that right?"

He laughed. "In a manner of speaking." He reached over to Harper and pulled down the zipper of her now very wrinkled dress. "How's this for a start?"

"It works." She stood before him in only her panties while she slid off his suit jacket then unbuttoned each shirt button slowly and methodically as he unknotted his tie.

He got to his belt before her and unfastened it while she took care of the zipper of his suit pants, and together they shimmied both those and his underwear off as he toed off his shoes and socks.

Once again Harper was left in underwear in those shoes, and despite himself, Noah grew instantly hard at the sight of her, so sexy and beautiful.

He looked down then up at her. "Sorry, I can't seem to help myself."

She grinned. "It's fine. But tell him it's look don't touch." She pointed to her feet. "Okay if I finally remove these?" She pulled back the covers and sat down on the edge of the bed.

He sighed. "I suppose if you must."

"Would you like to do the honors?"

His face lit up and he sat down next to her, motioning for her to put her foot in his now naked lap. "I'm gonna miss these," he said with a grin.

"Maybe if you're lucky they'll make a command performance at some point in time." Which would mean that they were still together, or at least sleeping together.

He smiled inwardly at this slight glimmer of hope. However he could water her garden, he was up for the task.

He fumbled slightly as he unbuckled the fine straps of her shoes, and once he'd removed them both, he massaged her feet. "I'd imagine they need this after withstanding hours teetering on those things."

She nodded. "The price of beauty is pain."

"I'm afraid sometimes the price of love is as well."

He motioned for her to make room so that he could join her but first helped her ease out of her panties.

"Just so you know this is going to take a tremendous amount of willpower to lie naked beside you like this. But I'm willing to undertake this mission because I believe in it."

She shrugged. "I'm not even sure at this point what the mission is, but I do remember my question: why'd you leave?"

The room was quiet but for the light hush of the furnace running. Now was the time for truths to come out, once and for all.

He took a deep breath.

"Right before I left, I found out that Matt had gotten Katie pregnant. Little Matt, my kid brother. Was he maybe twenty at the time? And bam, all of a sudden kicked in the gut with this reality. It scared the shit out of me. Even more so because of all the 'real world' stuff that was looming."

Wanting to run his fingers through her silky strands, he paused to pull the ponytail holder out of Harper's hair. They were facing each other, side by side, their bodies touching in some places but not in others. Despite the intensity of the discussion Noah wanted nothing more than to drag his cock along her slit to see if she was as wet as he hoped. But he had to refrain.

"I guess Matt's thing stirred up huge feelings of inadequacy in me due to my father leaving me when I was a toddler. All of a sudden, I felt like I must be exactly like my shitty father, unable to hold down a commitment. I thought I would jump out of my skin if I didn't put one foot in front of the other and keep on going."

He placed his hands on either side of her face, then gently placed a kiss on her forehead.

"And so I left."

He could hear Harper softly crying now and it broke his heart how much he'd hurt her. He pulled her into a hug, stroking her back to soothe her.

"Harper, I wrote you lengthy notes of explanation in my head all the time. I had conversations with you, detailing my motivations. But every time they seemed to fall short, so instead I did nothing. I convinced myself that you were better off without me, that I'd let you down and it was time to move on."

In between soft sobs, Harper prompted him for more answers. "But where did you go? What did you do?"

"I traveled for a long while. Worked on self-discovery at an ashram in India."

She wrinkled her nose. "And did you find yourself?"

He shrugged. "It's complicated. I mean yeah, it was one step on a crooked path to figuring my shit out. A really hot step, I might add. It made me appreciate air conditioning, that's for sure." A smile curled up one side of his mouth.

She frowned. "Dammit, Noah. Stop with the grinning. That smile always sucker punches me right in the solar plexus. How can a girl resist that thing?"

Did that mean she was finding him irresistible? Could

it be possible that she would consider a reconciliation? Did he dare hold out hope?

"So then what happened?"

"Eventually I came back to the States and started law school. It wasn't long after that when my mother became ill, and I needed to be honest with myself that I hated every minute of law school anyhow, so I withdrew."

"Do you regret it?"

He lifted his eyebrow. "Hell no. I wasn't cut out to be a lawyer. I'm too averse to conflict."

"Is that why you left me? To avoid conflict with me?"

She was avoiding eye contact with him, so he lifted her chin with his pointer finger, fixing his gaze on hers.

"The thing is, Harp, the crazy thing is, it had nothing to do with you. I know that doesn't help you at all. But it was all about me. I totally get that what I did was about the shittiest thing I could have done to you. It wrecked your self-esteem. At the time, I was too caught up in me to realize that. I needed so badly to get away. To escape my brother's fate.

"When Katie got pregnant, it scared the crap out of me. All of a sudden I watched my own life flickering by like on one of those movie reels they used to show at the cinema back during World War II. And it was me and you and a passel of kids and me with a lousy job and not being able to afford a wife let alone a kid, let alone a slew of them, and I don't know why it scared me so much. More than likely because of my father, because of what a complete dick he was, up and leaving my mom the way he did, with her having to support two kids on her lousy salary and how we always struggled and did without."

He ran his fingers through his hair, exasperated at himself for his lousy explanation. "So what was my response? I did the stupid thing: I ran from you before we got caught up with burden and responsibility and the real world in ways that I wasn't prepared to contemplate."

"But you didn't even include me in that discussion, Noah. You didn't give me a chance to have a say in things. You took my rights from me. And you took my boyfriend from me." She shook her head as if she was erasing that comment. "No. You took my world away from me. You and I had been together forever. It was always Harper and Noah. Noah and Harper. But then it was bye-bye Noah and to a certain extent bye-bye Harper. I didn't even know who I was. I was so lost without you. And heartbroken. And insulted. And truly disrespected. You didn't have the common decency to include me in your decision-making."

He leaned forward and tenderly clasped her face between his hands. "In some ways that's important, Harper. Don't you see? You and I didn't have a you and an I. We were a 'we.' We'd become one unit. I needed to figure out me. And I think you did as well. Had I stayed here, you never would have detached from me. And it's not that I didn't like to be so close to you—I loved it. But I knew in my gut that we needed to be two separate people before we could ever become one in a true sense of the word. And of course I knew leaving was the ultimate risk because the chances were strong that you'd never take me back. It was a risk I believed I had no choice but to take."

She frowned.

He pulled her close, locking eyes with hers. "I could never have been the man you needed when I was the boy I was. I needed to grow, to learn, to live before I could have understood what it meant to truly be the man you deserve, Harper. I hope you'll take that into consideration."

Chapter Twenty-Two

HARPER was struggling with all of Noah's revelations. They made so much sense if seen through the prism of his lens. But through hers, she was never able to see that. She only knew the hurt, pain, and rejection she'd experienced. And as much as she knew Noah, there was this internal struggle she didn't understand: all the things with his dad and his fears that he might be cut from the same cloth. She had no idea.

And the law school. Noah had talked about that for years. It was hard to fathom the change of heart.

"Betty said you left law school because your mother was sick."

He shook his head. "Not because, but when. The truth was I'd already reached a point where I knew it was time to let it go. I thought it was my dream, but it turns out it wasn't."

"I'm so sorry."

"About Mom? Or law school?"

"Both? But mostly your mom. She was a lovely woman."

"Yeah, well I'm sorry too about my mom. But don't lose any sleep over the law school bit. I wasn't cut out to be a lawyer. So much arguing. So much studying. It wasn't for me. I wasn't meant to be the next Clarence Darrow."

"You know something?" She twirled her fingers in Noah's chest hair.

"What?"

"I thought you were working like a minimum wage job at the inn. I had no idea it was yours. Is it something you want to continue?"

He pulled her closer. "Honestly at first, I thought I'd only try to dig the thing out of debt. My mother was a lovely person but she mismanaged the hell out of the place. I've worked hard these past several months to correct inefficiencies, consolidate debt, everything to make this place work. And in the process, I sort of fell in love with it."

"It agrees with you. I watched you working there. You can tell it makes you happy. And you're comfortable with it."

He smiled that half smile again. "I'm finding all sorts of familiar things have become particularly comfortable."

He pressed his hands on her bottom and pulled her toward him. There was no mistaking what he was talking about. Comfortable would be an understatement.

"But wait a minute," she said, holding up a finger. "One thing you haven't confessed to yet: Who is the boy on Facebook? And what is your relationship with his mother?"

"Wait—you were spying on my Facebook page? Does that mean you were stalking me?" He grinned and she poked her finger into his arm, hard. "Ouch! What was that for?"

"Just because. It's the least I can do to teach you a lesson."

"Oh, I've got all kinds of lessons I wouldn't mind

teaching you. Or vice versa. I'm a good student. I promise."

"You're still not answering me. The boy with the whipped cream beard."

Noah laughed. "You mean Tyler?"

"Tyler? Is this Matt's boy? I think that's the name Betty referred to."

"And my relationship with his mother is that she's my sister-in-law."

Harper blushed. "When I saw that picture of you with him, I thought you had left me because you got some other woman pregnant. I thought he was your son."

"Harps, do you seriously think I would have cheated on you?"

She pushed out her lower lip. "No, but I also never thought you would have abandoned me."

He pulled her to him. "Fair enough."

"You couldn't get more out of character than that."

He laughed quietly. "Probably knocking up some woman behind your back and leaving you for her would have trumped what I pulled." He pressed his lips to her forehead. "I'd hope you would have given me the benefit of the doubt. But I get it, Harps. You had no more benefit of the doubt left to give. Though I'm awfully surprised you hadn't heard through the grapevine about Matt and Katie."

"Maybe under other circumstances, I would have. But I shut out your family and everything to do with them. Everyone knew I was going to cut them off if they shared anything to do with you."

"Ouch."

"Did I mention how much that hurt me?"

"Maybe once or twice."

Harper's text dinged while they lay there. She grabbed

her phone from off of the nightstand.

"Let me make sure this isn't anything urgent," she said. "It's not like I get middle-of-the-night texts normally."

She held out her phone as she pressed her thumb to open the text.

"Who is it?"

"It's Danny,"

"The fly-eater?"

"Very funny."

"Seriously, Harper, I've been meaning to tell you something about him."

"Give me a sec," she said, holding up a finger. "Wait. This is really weird. This is really weird."

"Is everything okay?"

She shook he head. "It says it's from his wife." She read aloud from the text. "Listen, bitch. This is Danny's wife. I know about you. I've been reading Danny's messages. I know about all of his women. Let me tell you: if you ever fucking go near my husband again, you'll have me to answer to."

Harper's eyes opened wide. "What the hell?"

Noah reached for her hand in the dark. "That's what I wanted to let you know about. Only I wasn't quite sure how to break it to you."

"What are you talking about?"

"I was on my way to the men's room, and I overheard him having a phone conversation when you two were out together. I heard him talking intimately to someone on the phone and from the sounds of it, it seemed like it was a serious relationship."

"And you didn't let me know about it?"

He clasped her hand between his. "I wasn't exactly sure of the best way to break it to you. I mean if I went up and told you, you'd never have believed me, would you? You'd have accused me of being jealous or trying to break you up."

Harper was quiet while she mulled this. "You were jealous of him, though?" It was a statement, but she was asking as if it was a question.

He murmured into her neck. "Jealous doesn't even begin to touch what I was feeling toward that fly-eating little shit. First off, I didn't want him anywhere near you, and I had to bite my lip even though all I wanted to do was beat the crap out of him and tell him to stay away from you. When I found out he was likely two-timing you, I wanted to kill him. I knew that would be so hurtful to you and you didn't deserve to be hurt again. I'd already hurt you enough for a lifetime. I'm sorry to have kept it from you, but until I had better proof, I could never have convinced you. Do you forgive me?"

She sighed. "What bums me out is that I was so damned gullible."

"I'm not sure if I even want to know this, but did you have feelings for him?"

"Well, right now my feelings involve wanting to wrap my hands around his sneaky bastard throat," she said. "I mean, he seemed so nice and charming and cute and all. Though to be honest, there was something missing there. I didn't get any fireworks, even though I tried."

"Fireworks?"

"When we kissed. It didn't stir anything in me. It was kind of like kissing a brother."

Noah grinned. "You know I was hoping against hope you didn't carry a torch for him. When you described your kiss in my car that night as 'nice,' I was certain I still had a chance with you. I could tell it was your first kiss, and nobody can get too excited about a kiss that was 'nice' or 'pleasant.'"

"Good detective work." She sighed. "Yeah, try as I might, it simply didn't blow my skirt."

"Score one for the good guys, then. I'd like nothing more than to blow that skirt of yours."

"That makes us even then because you've got something I might be happy to blow—" She blurted out a laugh.

"You get no objections from me, babe." He wrapped his arms around her waist, pulling her tightly to him. "You gonna reply to that disgruntled wife of the fly-eater?"

Harper paused for a minute, pondering. "Nah. Let's let it dangle. He deserves that."

"So that leaves it up to me to stake my claim, then."

"Stake away, Noah. But don't do anything that's going to hurt me, okay? My heart can't take that ever again."

"I know I'm going to have to keep working hard to regain your trust, Harper. But I want you to know I'm going to be relentless in that pursuit. So don't for a second think I'm going to stop proving myself to you. Because I love you, Harper Landry. For that matter, I always have."

"It's only that for a long damned time you had a funny way of showing it."

"Try me now—I think I can persuade you."

She arched an eyebrow. "You think, do you?"

He nodded. "About that dry spell…"

"Ahhh," she said. "Of course. I think you'll need to water my garden on a fairly regular basis to prove that you're intentions are honorable."

"My hose is at the ready."

And they laughed with relief as Noah rolled her over to prove his point.

Thank you so much for reading **_Falling for Mr. Wrong_**! I hope you enjoyed it! If so, please help others find this book:

1. Help other people find this book by writing a review.

2. Sign up for my new releases email so you can find out about the next book as soon as it's available and get fun giveaways.
    http://eepurl.com/baaewn

3. Like my Facebook page.
    www.facebook.com/jennygardinerbooks

And I love to hear from readers! Let me know what you think about my books! You can write to me at jenny@jennygardiner.net, and visit me on the web at www.jennygardiner.net.

Keep reading for a sample from Falling for Mr. Maybe, the next book in the Falling for Mr. Wrong series.

Falling

for

Mr. Maybe

by Jenny Gardiner

Chapter One

GEORGIA Childress took an odd sort of pride in all the dinks and rust spots her fifteen-year-old chalk-yellow Volvo station wagon sported. Maybe they weren't exactly badges of honor, but each one had its own little story to tell, even if they did occasionally remind her of some of her more blond moments while driving in which she perhaps could have paid a little bit more attention while behind the wheel. And at the end of the day, they were a part of who Georgie was, like it or not.

The good news is nothing really bad ever happened in any of those episodes. Even the time she sort of backed out erratically and scraped bumpers with the mayor (four-inch-long black streak on the front right bumper) ended up being okay; Mayor Petrilli liked Georgie enough to hire her to petsit her two yellow Labs when she went on vacation for two weeks. Granted she did insist that she not take the dogs in her car, but nevertheless, it was all good.

Even that time she backed into her brother's best friend Max's ten-speed bike (ten-inch scrape caused by the bike's hand brakes along the center of the trunk), it worked out. Yeah, it did cost her a few hundred dollars in repairs, but he didn't stay mad at Georgie. For long.

Georgie had just gotten back into her car after taking a late-day stroll along the beach. Whenever she got a chance to take a break and sink her toes into the warm, fine sand along the shoreline, she did so. It was her happy place, listening to the repetitive swoosh of waves upon the shore. Walking along the beach helped her put life into perspective and gave her a sense of inner peace.

Summer was on the wane, and soon the beach landscape would take on an entirely different complexion and not be so welcoming to bare feet and tank tops. Although Georgie was happy to stroll beachside even with snow falling from the sky—unfortunately becoming more and more rare here in North Carolina—she was happiest on a day like today: wisps of cotton-candy clouds lacing the late-afternoon sky as the sun cast its warm melon glow across the sand.

It's one of the reasons she moved back to Verity Beach in the first place; something about the ocean called to her. Sometimes she swore she must have been a mermaid (better that than, say, a sea manatee, or a man-of-war jellyfish) in a past life, she loved the ocean so much. Although, yeah, that whole broken engagement in D.C. thing certainly impelled her homeward as well. Nothing like being dumped weeks before your betrothal to the man you thought loved you to send you scurrying back to a place of comfort and familiarity.

Georgie knocked the sand off of her feet and slid them back into her flipflops. She needed to get to the grocery store and pick up something to make for dinner, and it was getting late. Her tummy was rumbling and she freely admitted she was a slave to that demanding organ.

She put the key in the ignition, switched the radio to

her favorite station, and threw the car in reverse, accelerating out of her space maybe a little faster than necessary. Until she heard a loud crunch and slammed on the brakes.

"Crap," she said, throwing open her door (dinging the car door next to hers in the process) and walking to the back to see what had happened.

She crunched up her chin and pursed her lips as she took in the sight of a surfboard lopped in half, one side partially dangling by some strands of wood but hanging at a distinctly perpendicular angle to the other half of it, which seemed to have smushed into the back-end of the car next to her, leaving a fairly ugly dent in the vehicle.

Which was evidently owned by a sort of cute guy with a really huge scowl on his face.

"Hey lady," he shouted, shaking his fist. "What the fuck? You murdered my board!"

Which Georgie knew was her cue to apologize profusely, even as she stared at the guy, whose wet suit was stripped down to his lean hips, exposing a beautiful, tanned chest with strong pecs, dusted with golden hair, which complemented the shoulder-length dirty blond hair on his head and the sexy needs-a-shave scruff on his handsome face.

"Oh my god, I am sooooooo sorry," Georgie said, reaching to lift the surfboard as if she could just force the two pieces back together. She could not. "I don't know how I missed seeing that."

He was nodding his head as if in a catatonic state while flailing his arms in a fit of pique. "Any more than you could have missed a damned atom bomb dropping and the commensurate mushroom cloud," he said, his eyes wide with what might have been incredulity. "I mean what about the damned board could you not have seen when you were backing out? It's six freaking feet long. That's like not seeing a grown man in your rearview mirror."

Georgie knit her brow, mortified but also kind of indignant because it was as if he thought she'd done it on purpose.

"Except this was sideways, not up and down." She sort of shifted her hands in a horizontal then vertical manner to demonstrate.

He cocked his head, as if he was trying to grasp if she'd really just said that.

"I'm not going to dignify that daft reply with a response."

"Look, again, I'm really so very sorry," she said. "I don't know how I missed it. I was backing up. There was a glare in my mirror I think, the sun was reflecting off of something and it sort of blinded me for a second, and then, I don't know, your car was back there and it was at a weird angle I guess, and shit, look what I did to that, too." Georgie nodded at the damaged car.

She grabbed her purse from the car and quickly whipped out a checkbook. "Maybe can I just write you a check and we can not report this to my insurance? I don't know that I can afford another increase this year."

He sized up her car, which was downright riddled with pockmarks, much to her current embarrassment. It was the only time she really didn't feel so great about all the dinks.

"Gee, ya think?" he said.

She rifled through her bag for a pen. "Just tell me how much to replace it and well—" she licked her finger and tried to wipe away the marks on the back of his car, but she knew damned well they weren't tiny bumper marks but an actual dent. "Well, that too." She pointed at it.

"Again, I feel really badly about that. I don't know what happened."

He was shaking his head, and if she wasn't mistaken, she wondered if perhaps he was about to throw-up. He had that sort of green-around-the-gills appearance of someone so upset it was a distinct possibility. "You can't pay me enough."

She stopped and looked up, pen in hand at the ready. "What do you mean I can't pay you enough?"

"It's one-of-a-kind," he said. "I made it myself."

Georgie blanched. What were the chances? She couldn't just plow into a run-of-the-mill Walmart-special surfboard. No. It had to be a bespoke one. If that didn't beat it all.

"Well, crap," she said. "Now I feel even worse." Her eyes started to moisten and damn, if she didn't hate when she cried. She tried to wipe away the nascent tears with her shoulders, as if pretending she was just itching something on her face. But the thing is, she was one of those criers. A big ugly messy one, once she got going. And sure enough it was like her eyes were leaking, the tears started coming so fast. And with that came a couple of forlorn sobs, so pitiful she was sure she sounded like a dying hyena.

She set her checkbook onto the roof of his car then dug back into her purse in search of a tissue and pulled out one that had a clumped-up wad of chewing gum stuck to it, bunched the thing up, and blew her nose, taking care to not stick the gum to her nostrils.

"Here I was just going to enjoy this lovely day and that sunset, and it was just so beautiful, it reminded me of peppermint and Christmas and deliciousness and now—" She looked at him and he had that look that men sometimes get when they wish they could find an off switch for a woman but know that one doesn't exist, kind of quizzical yet annoyed, all tinged with anger. She hated that look; it reminded her of her father just before he would light off on her mother and scream and yell and pound his fists into the wall, sometimes so hard he put holes into the drywall. And that memory made her eyes water up even more, particularly because it evoked her parents broken marriage, which then stirred up memories of her own marriage, which never happened, and the next thing she knew she was leaning against the bumper of her beat-up old station wagon, bawling her eyes out and this strange man with the broken surfboard was leaning over her trying to calm her down.

"Look, lady, don't worry about it," he said. "I'll figure it out."

Between sobs she tried to speak. "But you made it. I can't even go buy you another."

"It'll be fine," he said, awkwardly rubbing her hair as if she was an excitable pooch that needed to be calmed down. "I was going to make a new one anyway."

She stopped crying for a minute and gave him a hopeful smile, which contrasted mightily with her tear-stained cheeks. She suspected she looked like a kid who just shattered his mother's family heirloom vase into a thousand pieces and the mom says not to worry, she can glue it back together. "You were?"

He furrowed his brow as he glanced at his murdered surfboard. "Yeah, in fact that was what I was planning to start working on this week," he said. "This one was getting old. Worn out."

She looked to see if maybe he'd crossed his fingers.

"Are you sure?"

"Um, yeah. Yeah. Of course."

She gave another tear-swipe with her shoulders, realizing too late that she didn't even have fabric from her tank top to catch the tears and snot, and they both streaked across her still-tanned shoulders in a most inelegant manner. Oooh, she must've been a sight for sore eyes.

"Well please, let me write a check so you can fix everything, okay?" Her fingers trembled as she scrawled out an amount on her check, not even bothering to ask his name, instead leaving it blank. "If you need anything more, my phone number's there." She pointed at her check.

His eyebrows were ski-sloped toward his nose. He did not look particularly happy.

"Yeah, sure," he said, shoving the check into his pocket. He leaned over and looked at her face intensely, sort of making Georgie feel uncomfortable, like he thought maybe she was going to walk straight on into the ocean and keep on walking till she was completely submerged, never to be seen again. "You okay?"

Which wasn't such a bad idea. If she were part mermaid, this would be the time to prove it. But that wasn't her style. She was certainly not a quitter. Besides, Georgie really hated being the center of anyone's attention, so she shrugged it off, waving her hand dismissively. "Hey, the good news is that," she said, nodding toward the board, "didn't happen out there." She pointed toward the ocean. "And it's not covered in your blood right? Way better my little fender-bender did this than a shark bite. Amiright?" She cracked a grin as she tried to make light of the situation.

The bummer on top of it everything else was that the yummy orzo lemon meatballs she had planned to make after she went to the grocery store were no longer going to be on the menu for dinner; she'd lost her appetite with all the drama. So much for that.

Instead she smoothed out the pout that threatened to freeze on her face, then cupped her hand in a tiny wave as she got back into her car, pulling away ever-so-carefully so as to not create any more disasters.

Chapter Two

SPENCER Willoughby wasn't sure exactly what had just hit him, figuratively-speaking. He knew for sure what had quite literally hit his board and his car—a beat-up, piece of shit vehicle driven by a whacked-out woman who somehow managed to make *him* feel badly that she'd trashed his Petie. Petie was his term of endearment for the beloved surfboard he crafted lovingly from his own two hands, the very board he'd ridden twice daily for the past three years.

For a second he tucked away his outrage to try to digest what had just transpired. Sheesh, that was the weirdest thing he'd experienced in a long while. Crazy lady surfboard killer cries and makes him feel bad. What the ever-loving hell?

He kept looking at Petie, his hands caressing the smooth edges, his eyes not wanting to make contact with the harshly-fractured scene of the crime that only drove home to him the board's premature demise.

He felt like crying. His plans for the afternoon had been so simple: all he'd wanted to do was take in a couple of nice waves at sunset on a glorious Indian summer kind of day, have a couple of beers, and call it a night. But now, shit, now not only could he not surf today, he couldn't surf on the very board it had taken him months to make. That sucked massively.

The good news is he was nearly finished with one he'd started working on a while ago, although it was originally intended to be a gift for his kid brother Nate for Christmas. He knew, deep down, it would be kind of dickish of him to keep it for himself. But then again, it's not like his brother would use it in late December. Oh, hell, who was he kidding? Even Spencer would use it in late December. That's why God invented wetsuits, right?

His mind kept going back to the crazy lady who was bawling in front of him just minutes ago. How weird was that? He was the one with the dead board yet there he was left comforting her as if in her hour of need. He scratched his head, wondering how that turn of events came about.

And also he wondered why he kept thinking about those aquamarine eyes of hers, which reminded him of tropical tide pools when they filled with tears like they had. Something about those eyes just pulled him in, despite his anger. Or maybe it was just that smoking rack she was sporting. She wasn't a small girl by any stretch, and her luscious breasts complimented her size quite nicely, two perfectly-sized globes tucked into that hot pink tank so perfectly. Here he was so pissed at that strange woman yet all he could think about was how much he'd love to get his hands on those things.

At least his priorities were straight. He laughed.

Meanwhile the amount of the check she gave him was pretty insignificant. It wasn't going to cover the cost of replacement wood, let alone the time it would take him to craft another board, and certainly not the dent in the back end of his car. Good thing he could get his neighbor Ben to bang out the dent, maybe even do a little quickie paint

Jenny Gardiner

touch-up. The car was old and beat-up anyhow, so that wasn't his primary concern. It was simply how the hell was he going to surf until he finished his next board? He'd gotten spoiled with his baby. Now he was going to have to go back to one of his old store-bought surfboards, which was a bummer. Ah well, he was nothing if not flexible. He was going to just have to deal with it.

He pulled the woman's check out of his pocket and read it, realizing he hadn't even learned her damned name. He squinted at the small print till he saw it: Georgia Childress. Huh. She sort of looked like a Georgia. Tall and strong, built like she knew how to take care of her body. He liked a woman like that. He stared at her phone number, wondering if maybe he should write that down, just in case. It was weird, her giving him a check. Who even writes checks in this day and age? She could've just Venmo'd him the money.

He pulled out his phone and snapped a quick picture of the check, phone number and all. That way if anything came up he'd know how to get hold of her. Although right now the only thing that seemed like it was coming up was becoming a bit too obvious pressing up against the crotch of his wetsuit. Seriously, just thinking about her tits had done this to him? What guy gets his board killed, his car dented, and can only think about how he might be able to get into the pants of the perpetrator? He laughed. Scratch that—plenty of men.

He dragged his hand over the day-old (ish) beard on his chin and shook his head. He knew he had to put those thoughts out of his mind immediately. He didn't come here to get involved with a woman, ditzy or not. He came here to get away from responsibility in all forms, and, well, crap, usually hopping on his surfboard served to clear his mind from such emotional pollutants. Looked like today he was just going to have to pretend this never happened, because that seemed the easiest way to purge the hot blond surfboard killer from his besotted mind.

He took one more look at his broken board.

Good luck with that, he thought, shaking his head. Why did he have the nagging feeling she was going to be harder to cleanse from his thoughts than the others were?

Falling for Mr. Maybe

coming January 9, 2018.

About the Author

Jenny Gardiner is the author of #1 Kindle Bestseller *Slim to None* and the award-winning novel *Sleeping with Ward Cleaver*. Her latest works are the *It's Reigning Men* series, the *Royal Romeos* series and her new *Falling for Mr. Wrong* series, beginning with *Falling for Mr. Wrong* and the upcoming *Falling for Mr. Maybe.* She also published the memoir *Winging It: A Memoir of Caring for a Vengeful Parrot Who's Determined to Kill Me,* now re-titled *Bite Me: a Parrot, a Family and a Whole Lot of Flesh Wounds*; the novels *Anywhere but Here*; *Where the Heart Is*; the essay collection *Naked Man on Main Street*, and *Accidentally on Purpose* and *Compromising Positions* (writing as Erin Delany); and is a contributor to the humorous dog anthology *I'm Not the Biggest Bitch in This Relationship*.

Her work has been found in Ladies Home Journal, the Washington Post, Marie-Claire.com, and on NPR's Day to Day. She was also a columnist for Charlottesville's Daily Progress for over a decade, and is the Volunteer Coordinator for the Virginia Film Festival.

She has worked as a professional photographer, an orthodontic assistant (learning quite readily that she was not cut out for a career in polyester), a waitress (probably her highest-paying job), a TV reporter, a pre-obituary writer, as well as a publicist to a United States Senator (where she first learned to write fiction). She's photographed Prince Charles (and her assistant husband got him to chuckle!), Elizabeth Taylor, and the president of

Uganda. She and her family and menagerie of pets now live a less exotic life in Virginia.

Visit Jenny at her website and sign up for her newsletter, her blog, or find her on Facebook and Twitter. And every blue moon she'll post adorable pictures of her pets on Instagram as @thejennygardiner.